W9-ATZ-151

Breaking Out

Also by Barthe DeClements

Nothing's Fair in Fifth Grade

Sixth Grade Can Really Kill You

How Do You Lose Those Ninth Grade Blues?

Seventeen and In-Between

I Never Asked You to Understand Me

Double Trouble

No Place for Me

The Fourth Grade Wizards

Five-Finger Discount

Monkey See. Monkey Do.

Breaking Out

Barthe DeClements

Delacorte Press

Published by
Delacorte Press
Bantam Doubleday Dell Publishing Group, Inc.
666 Fifth Avenue
New York, New York 10103

Library of Congress Cataloging in Publication Data

DeClements, Barthe.
    Breaking out / by Barthe DeClements.
        p.   cm.
    Summary: As thirteen-year-old Jerry enters junior high
school, he continues to adjust to the fact that his father is
in prison for theft. Sequel to *Five-Finger Discount* and *Monkey See. Monkey Do.*
    ISBN 0-385-30503-6
    [1. Prisoners' families—Fiction.   2. Fathers and sons—
Fiction.   3. Schools—Fiction.]   I. Title.
PZ7.D3584Br   1991
[Fic]—dc20   91-6779
                                                         CIP
                                                          AC

Manufactured in the United States of America

November 1991

10   9   8   7   6   5   4   3   2   1

BVG

This book is dedicated to my delightful brother, Jim, who brought me dates when I was young and lent me his convertible when he went off to war.

I wish to acknowledge my indebtedness to my son, Christopher Greimes, and my daughter, Nicole Southard, for editing the manuscript. I wish to thank Sue Anne Torres for allowing me to quote from her story, "Being Six"; George Selvidge for sharing his expertise on TV commercials; and my grandson, Scott Southard, for his feedback on the manuscript in progress. I wish also to express my thanks to Rae Ann Engdahl and her students and Morrie Schneider and his students at Kamiakin Junior High for their contributions to this book.

Contents

1	Rip Off	1
2	Buffalo Butt	9
3	Laugh It Off	17
4	Losing It	25
5	Warm Bones	33
6	Big Mouth	41
7	Tryout	51
8	Convict's Kid	57
9	Way to Go	65
10	Grungy Thief	73
11	Sorry	81
12	One Smokin' Buggy	89
13	Action!	97
14	She's Not Perfect	105
15	A Chip off the Old Block	113
16	The End of Holy Grace	123

Breaking Out

1

Rip Off

"But, Jerry, this is your last day before school starts," Mom said. "Wouldn't you like to see a movie?"

"Naw, that's okay," I told her. "You guys go."

Mom tilted her head at me, pleading silently, while Willard slapped his cap on his bald head and marched to the door. "If we're going, let's go."

She shot me one last wistful glance before following Willard out of the house. He didn't care if I came or not. He just goes to keep Mom happy. He doesn't even like movies.

What Willard likes is money. Not to spend, that's for sure. Just to count. The only time you catch Willard smiling is after he's closed his restaurant and is thumbing through his take at the cash register. I'll be vacuuming the carpet, Mom will be filling salt shakers, the last waitress will be hauling out dirty tablecloths, and Willard, Willard will be at the register with his calculator, stacks of money, glinty eyes, and greedy grin.

Willard's grin fades when Mom buttons the collar of her coat and I put out my hand for my evening's pay. I

1

only work on nights he's shorthanded, so I've made it a practice to get paid on the spot. Yet every single time, he stares down at me and says, "What do you want?"

"I want to get paid," I answer.

Then he says, "Your mother shared her tips with you, didn't she?"

I used to explain that every waitress shares tips with her busboy. That didn't seem to cut any ice with him, so now I just stand with my hand out until he puts the money in it. He acts as if it's an imposition to give me anything, as if I should be happy to contribute to the family. I buy my own clothes and sometimes even my own dinner when nobody's home. I figure that's contributing enough.

I don't like Willard much and I don't think he likes me. It's probably not necessary to like your stepfather, especially when you love your own dad. My problem is that my real dad's in prison.

I thought about this later in my tree house, where I'd gone to bed in my sleeping bag. I was up there because I didn't want to be around when Willard got home. I had my arms crossed under my head and was looking at the sky and thinking about my old man, wondering if he had a window in his cell where he could see the stars.

My dad isn't like Willard. My dad's funny and friendly and warm and a con artist with sticky fingers. He's got street smarts but I wish he had Willard's plain, everyday sense so he could figure out consequences before he did stupid things. Things like lifting a carton of cigarettes in a grocery store where he'd taken me and some kids in my class after a field trip. Swiping cigarettes isn't a felony, but my old man was on parole, so it was back to the lockup for him.

2

I guess most kids'd be fascinated to see someone's dad hauled off in a cop car. And they'd be jumping up and down to be the first to spread the news. Only kids with guts like Grace and Summer and Clayton would hang by you. Ordinary guys like Pete would follow their moms' advice and stay away from you so they wouldn't get contaminated.

What worried me that September night before school started was how the new kids at junior high were going to take me. Would the kids in my old sixth-grade class pass the word around about my dad? Or would all the seventh-graders be so nervous about their locker combinations and how to go to the bathroom and get over to the gym on time that they wouldn't be interested in my dad?

I curled up on my side in my sleeping bag and fell asleep still worrying. It must have been about midnight when I was jerked awake by the closing of a car door. I didn't wake up because the car door was slammed. Grace's brother, Matt, always slams his. I woke up because I heard a car door being closed quietly. Why would anyone do that in my neighborhood?

I lay in my sleeping bag for a few minutes, trying to figure out what was going on. Then I told myself, "Crawl out and look, stupid."

Crawling halfway out of my bag, I leaned over the edge of the platform and peered through the tree branches at the curb in front of my house. Nothing. Only Willard's old station wagon was there and it wasn't moving. I was about to pull back when a light turned on somewhere below me. It was a faint light, and I had to inch around the platform toward the Elliotts' house before I found its source.

3

The light was coming from inside Matt's car, which was parked in his driveway. At first I thought he must have a girl with him and I couldn't figure out why he'd be making out in his own yard. But when I leaned way down and turned my head sideways, I could see a bald head on the driver's side and a beam from a flashlight shining on the dashboard.

Everyone in the Elliott family has thick black hair. Whoa! Matt's car was getting hot-wired.

I kicked off the bottom of my sleeping bag and was halfway down the ladder and turning my head to spot the ground when I caught a flash of my bare white butt. Rats. I climbed back up, snaked into my jeans, leapt off the ladder midway, and ran across the wet grass and around the Elliotts' garage to their back door.

It wasn't till then that it dawned on me that the thief, only a few yards away, would be able to hear anything the Elliotts heard. Cupping my body over my fist to muffle the sound of my knocking, I waited, my heart beating. No sound from the car by the side of the house. But no sound from inside the house either.

I pressed around my hand again and thumped the door some more. I waited. Silence all around. Must be a dumb thief to take so long to start an engine. I thumped and waited again. Not a stir inside the house. This wasn't going to work. Gravel on a window might, but the only gravel was in the driveway.

I stood on one bare foot and then the other, trying to figure out what to do. Thump harder, I guessed, and pray the thief wouldn't come running around the porch to whack me on the side of the head. I pounded the door. Waited. Shivered with fear that my luck might run out. Nothing! Not a sound.

4

The key to my back door was up in the tree inside my jacket pocket. I'd just decided to go get it and call the cops from my house when a shadow appeared in the Elliotts' kitchen. I squinted at the door window until I heard a lock click and then I pushed inside before a light could be turned on.

"Shhh." I silently closed the door behind me.

"What's up?" Matt whispered.

"Your car's getting ripped off."

He had me shoved aside and the door flung open before I could warn him that the thief wasn't a kid. I heard Matt hit the gravel just as the engine started up. When I reached the driveway, he was racing after his car, which was roaring down the road.

It was a hopeless chase, and it wasn't long before he stumbled back into the yard. "Get my dad, will ya?" Matt bent over, gasping for breath.

I spun around, sprinted for his back door, and nearly smashed into Reverend Elliott as he was coming out. If I had, it would have knocked me flat because he's as big as a grizzly bear. "What's going on?" he asked me.

"Matt's car's been stolen."

The Reverend rushed out to the driveway and clapped his big paw on Matt's shoulder. "Are you all right?"

"Sure, but I think the guy's heading for the bridge. If he doesn't go on the freeway, we might catch him."

"I'll get the keys."

The Reverend got the keys, then ran for the garage and his Toyota with Matt close behind him. I stood by the garage doors wondering what I should do. "Jerry, tell Mrs. Elliott to phone the police," the Reverend hollered out of the car window as the Toyota passed me.

I went around to the Elliotts' back porch, slower this

time. Just as I was knocking on the open door, Grace and her mom came into the kitchen. Mrs. Elliott was bundled up in a purple bathrobe, and her head, poking out of all that flannel, looked like a skinned onion studded with bobby pins.

She frowned at my bare chest.

I tried to explain that I had been sleeping in my tree house when someone closing a car door woke me up and I hadn't wanted to waste time dressing before I warned Matt that his car was being stolen.

"Stolen!" Mrs. Elliott flipped on the outside light, marched across the porch, craned her neck around the corner of the house, and looked down the empty driveway.

"When was it stolen?" she asked me after coming back in the kitchen.

"A few minutes ago. Your husband wants you to call the police."

"The police? I don't know the license number of the car. I don't know where—"

Grace pointed her mother toward the hall. "Matt has a dozen pictures of the car on his bedroom wall."

Grace'd looked sleepy when she first came into the kitchen, but now her blue eyes were round with excitement. "Weren't you scared to climb out of your tree house with the robber so close?"

"I gave it a thought," I said, "but I wanted to wake up Matt before the guy got away."

"That was nice of you. My brother'd die if he lost his car."

"Ya, I guess he would." It was all I could think of to say. I was becoming conscious again of my bare chest and of Grace's nightgown.

6

So was Mrs. Elliott when she returned. "I've called the police and that's all we can do for now. You'd better run on home, Jerry, and get some sleep. Junior high starts tomorrow."

"We know, Mom." Grace followed me to the door. "Matt will sure appreciate what you did," she said to me.

I nodded good-bye before I went down the steps. It was too bad Mrs. Elliott didn't appreciate what I'd done too. I knew she didn't want Grace hanging around with me any more than Pete's mom did, but she could have at least said "Thanks."

I was still mumbling to myself about Mrs. Elliott's ungratefulness when I crawled back in my sleeping bag. Then another thought hit me. How come it was Matt's car that was stolen? Maybe one of the ex-cons Dad had hanging around when he lived here had done it. Rattler and Louis were both car thieves, but they were supposed to be in jail.

The last time I'd seen Rattler, his forehead was pretty high. Could he have gone bald in a year? Rolling over on my side, I laid my head on my arm and folded my legs up to my stomach. I fell asleep hoping I wouldn't have to apologize to Mrs. Elliott for my dad's friends.

2

Buffalo Butt

I waited on the sidewalk in front of Grace's house, checking my watch every few seconds. I'd wanted to be at the bus stop early, but now there was barely enough time to make it. I was about to move on when Grace came out her front door, slammed it hard, and stomped down the steps.

She was wearing a dorky-looking plaid skirt and a long-sleeved blue blouse. "You think it's going to snow today?" I asked.

"Don't say anything," she said. "This isn't my idea. It's my mother's."

"They're your mom's clothes?"

"Very funny!"

I hadn't meant to be funny. I really thought they might be her mom's clothes. They didn't look like anything a junior high kid would wear. Not anything I'd seen in the stores anyway.

"What happened to your brother's car last night? Did the police find it?"

9

"No, nobody did." She was dragging along the sidewalk with her head down.

"Let's speed it up a little," I said. "I don't want to miss the bus on the first day."

"I don't care if I never get to school."

Something in me made me bend over and peer into Grace's face. Her reddened eyes were swimming with tears. She jerked her head to the side. "Don't look at me."

"Jeez, okay," I told her, and we walked the rest of the way to the bus in silence.

Grace got on first, and I expected her to head for the rear of the bus, where all her friends usually sat. Instead she halted halfway down the aisle, causing me to stumble. I checked to see what had stopped her and saw there weren't any girls giggling in the back. The seats were filled with boys.

"Yo, Johnson!" Clayton waved his arm in the air.

I gave him a smile and a brief wave before I sat down beside Grace. "Why don't you go sit with them?" she asked. "The guys have obviously taken over the place."

"Pete's sitting with them," I said.

"So?"

"What do you mean 'so'? His mom transferred him out of my class last year to keep him away from me."

"Oh, she's a pain just like my . . ." Grace didn't finish her sentence. She turned to stare out the window.

Pete's mom *was* a jerk just like Grace's mom. Only Grace's mom could get overruled by the Reverend. As the bus zipped by the tree-lined sidewalks, I wondered why he hadn't rescued Grace from her dorky outfit and then I wondered how seventh-graders got treated in junior high.

10

"Do you think they'll try to initiate us?" I asked Grace. She shot me an evil grin. "Maybe the ninth-graders will give you a swirly."

The Welcome to Riverside Junior High letter we'd gotten in August said school would commence with a general assembly at eight thirty. It was eight twenty when we pulled into the parking lot. I noticed all the short kids were hurrying toward the gym, while the older kids were strolling along yakking to each other. I was as big as most of the older guys because I'd grown two inches since spring and had swum all summer in the Pilchuck River.

Pete and Russell moved ahead of me, and I watched them go through the gym doors. In grade school Pete had seemed tall. Now he just looked skinny, and Russell was his same old blubbery self.

There were large cardboard signs tacked to the bleachers. The left bleachers were for ninth-graders, the front of the right bleachers were for eighth-graders, and the ones near the doors were for seventh-graders. Grace stopped to sit with one of her old girlfriends on the bottom bench. Pete and Russell climbed about halfway up before they sat down.

I caught Pete glancing at me as I started up the bleachers. When he saw I was watching, he pretended he was busy talking to Russell. I passed them and took one of the empty places on a top bench.

In fifth grade Pete and I had been pals. We'd horsed around at Grace's birthday party, hammed it up in plays, and creamed everybody at basketball. Then in sixth grade he saw my dad being hauled away by the cops. He never spoke to me after that, and I have to admit it hurts.

"Students, may I have your attention?" A thin man in

11

rimless glasses was standing at the microphone. "May I . . ."

Whatever he said next never reached the bleachers because the microphone went dead. The teachers, who were sitting behind him, craned their necks to inspect the wires running under their chairs. A burly one in sweats hopped out of his seat and plugged two cords together.

Clayton sat down beside me, shaking his head at the gym floor. "Real organized."

The thin man blew into the microphone. It worked. "May I have the gymnasium quiet, please? First I'd like to introduce myself to our new students. I'm Mr. Ratch, your vice principal."

There was a low groan from the ninth-grade section.

Ratch hurried on to introduce the principal, Mrs. Mc-Cann. She was the big woman in a red-flowered dress sitting at the end of the first row. Her head was held high, her back was straight, and her left hand was poised in front of her neck with her thumb and first finger touching her collarbone. She merely nodded to acknowledge the introduction.

"I bet nobody messes with her," Clayton whispered.

"Now I would like to present our new faculty member." Mr. Ratch checked the paper in his hand. "Ms. Thornsbury is a first-year teacher who will be taking over the home-ec department. Will you please stand, Ms. Thornsbury."

Ms. Thornsbury stood. She was the mousy thing in the back row.

Next Mr. Ratch had the PE teachers, the math teachers, the biology teacher, and the French teacher stand. A moan passed through the crowd when the second social studies teacher, Mrs. Beasley, rose from her chair. I sat

12

up straight to get a good look at her. "Who's she?" I asked Clayton.

"That's Beatrice Beasley. Old B.B. Buffalo Butt."

"I hope I don't get her."

"Pray," Clayton said. "She teaches seventh-grade Washington State history. My brother warned me about her."

After B.B. sat down, Mr. Ratch started on the English teachers. I was about to slouch back against the wall when a name he called was drowned out by whistles from the ninth-grade section. The teacher gave the guys a smile as she stood up. Mr. Ratch scowled. "*Please* hold your appreciation until all our teachers have been introduced."

I raised an eyebrow at Clayton.

He grinned. "Suzy Castle. She's got the drama club and acts in plays in Seattle."

"What a fox," I mumbled.

"Ya, but a little round in the legs and arms."

That was okay with me, because she was a little round in some other places too.

Mr. Ratch ended the assembly by telling the seventh-graders to read their handbooks and reminding the whole student body about the dress code. Cutoffs were out, shorts were okay if they covered the upper thighs and were hemmed, no T-shirts advertising beer or liquor, and no bare feet. Most of the guys were dressed like me, white T-shirt and jeans. Some were in shorts. A lot of the girls wore shorts. Nobody was dressed like Grace.

Clayton and I compared schedules before we got up from our seats. We both had math first period, but not in the same room. Washington State history was the only

13

subject we had together. "See you third period," Clayton said, heading down the bleachers.

When I got to the history class, I saw Summer dropping her book bag on a desk in the third row. Russell had spotted her, too, and was heading for the seat behind her, but I beat him to it.

"Hi, Johnson. Oh, and hi there, Summer. I didn't see you." He slid his fat stomach under the desk across from her as if that's where he'd wanted to be all along.

Summer turned around to me. "You sure have a neat tan."

"Yours is neat too. And where are your glasses?"

She poked a finger toward her green eyes. "Contacts."

"Neat." That's all I could think of to say. Without her glasses sliding down her nose, the full impact of Summer was hitting me, and I had trouble coming up with conversation.

Russell broke into the silence by tilting his head toward Summer's legs. "Great shorts."

"Thanks." She barely glanced at Russell. I think she remembered that he'd hassled her in sixth grade when she was new and bewildered. Not that Summer isn't always a little shy.

Clayton took the seat next to me. "You find out who the teacher is yet?"

While I shook my head no, Grace plunked her bag on the desk behind Clayton. I noticed she sat down quickly, hiding most of her long skirt under her bottom. She'd rolled up her sleeves and unbuttoned the top button of her blouse, but it hadn't helped much. "What're you guys talking about?" she asked.

"Who we're going to have for a teacher," I told her, but I don't think she heard my answer.

She was too busy taking in Summer's sleeveless pink turtleneck and bare legs.

Just at that moment the teacher walked in the door with a handful of papers, stopped in front of the room to stare at us until everyone hushed, and then marched up to the blackboard. Before she'd chalked on the first letter of her name, Clayton dropped his chin onto the heel of his hand and muttered through his fingers, "Buffalo Butt."

3

Laugh It Off

After Mrs. Beasley finished writing her name on the board, she placed all her papers on her desk except one. She held that one in front of her face and stood up real straight like she was trying to keep her belly from bulging out. She couldn't do anything about her hind end, though. It rode behind her like a caboose.

"Auchinson, Steven," she called out.

A blond spiky-haired kid raised his hand. She peered at him before she went on to the next name.

"Day, Summer."

Summer raised her hand.

Mrs. Beasley stared at her paper. "Summer Day?"

I could see the blush spreading down Summer's neck as Mrs. Beasley lowered her paper. "Summer Day? Your parents must have been hippies." Mrs. Beasley gave a little laugh. Nobody else did. How rude can a teacher get?

The only other weird name in the room was Lonewolf. He was the stubby kid who sat in front of Russell. When Mrs. Beasley called out, "Lonewolf, John," I waited for another crack. But she just peered at him a little longer than she had at the rest of us and then went on to "Sorenson, Aaron."

After role call was finished, Mrs. Beasley gave us her "expectations." Like expecting us to be sitting quietly in our seats when the bell rang and remembering to have our history book, three-ring binder, pen, and paper with us. Any student who forgot to bring "his or her essential materials" to class would receive an F for the day. In an effort to impress these expectations on us, Mrs. Beasley hovered over us a few seconds with her eyes opened wide. We were impressed.

She had Arnold and Russell pass out the books that were on the front table, told us to write our names in them, and warned us that we would be fined for each torn or mutilated page at the end of the year. We were responsible for purchasing a new book from Mr. Ratch if we lost the one she gave us or if it was stolen from our hall lockers. "Your lockers aren't safes," she said, "so don't keep your valuables in them."

I was so bummed by the time she finished her threats and told us to read chapter one in our books, I just flopped mine open and stared at the print. I was even more bummed after I forced myself to read five pages. The chapter was titled "The Lewis and Clark Expedition," but it was mostly about President Jefferson worrying about our country's enemies and false friends and how he was going to trick them by sneaking an exploration into the Northwest. I read the part twice about Jefferson getting Congress to buy Louisiana from France. Did that mean France was one of the enemies or a false friend?

I stretched my neck, wishing teachers would explain

clearly what had gone on and not expect you to tear it out from pages of tiny print. I sneaked a glance at Clayton. It looked like he was at the end of the chapter. Clayton's smart. He probably had Jefferson's problems all figured out.

A long, red fingernail tapped on page six of my book. I stared up into Mrs. Beasley's doughy face. "Let's keep our attention on our work," she said before moving down the aisle. Her sickening perfume hung behind her, stuffing up my nose and making me sneeze twice. I wiped the drops off my book with the side of my arm and went back to Jefferson choosing Captain Clark and Meriwether Lewis to lead a group of adventurers from the U.S. Army. How had they figured out who was an "adventurer" and who wasn't?

When the bell rang ending the history period, we all clapped our books closed and popped out of our seats. "Just a minute, stu-dents." Mrs. Beasley held her arm in the air.

We froze in our places.

"You don't leave until I dismiss you." She paused while I wiggled. She better not make me late to PE.

"Before tomorrow I expect everyone to have finished reading chapter one and be ready for a class discussion. You are dismissed."

I made a beeline for the door. The gym was way over on the north side of the building. Following my school map, I tunneled through the crowded halls as fast as I could. The littlest kids got the worst of the traffic jam. The ninth-graders just shoved them out of the way.

I was out of breath by the time I reached the gym, but there was nothing going on. A bunch of seventh-graders milled around the floor while a man with skinny legs and

19

a woman with brawny legs stood under a basketball hoop poring over long sheets of paper. I saw Pete on the other side of the gym talking to Eric. Kathy was standing near them. They were the only ones I spotted from our old elementary school.

The woman PE teacher stepped forward, announced that she was Ms. Kraft, and asked us to listen for our names. Every other student she called was to go to the right wall. The rest were to stand by the left wall. My name was the third one called, and I went to the right wall. Kathy's was the fifth. She took a place a couple yards away from me. I didn't know if it was because she didn't want to associate with me or wanted to be near another girl.

When John Lonewolf's name was called, he chose a place beside me. That took some pressure off while I listened for the *Ms*. "Pete McCartney!" Ms. Kraft yelled, and Pete ran over to the left wall while my hunched shoulders relaxed with relief.

Ms. Kraft led my group into the locker room, passed out little yellow slips with our locker combinations, waited while we experimented with our locks, and then took us out to the field for a game of baseball. I got to play first base. Lonewolf was the catcher on my side. His arm shot out like a frog's tongue as he snagged every strike and foul ball into his glove. I guess stubbiness pays when you're squatting behind home plate.

Lonewolf and I walked back to the gym together, and Ms. Kraft caught up with us before we got to the doors. "You two looked good out there," she said. "I hope you're both going to turn out for baseball in the spring."

"Will they take seventh-graders?" I wanted to know.

20

"Sure, the only team you can't get on before eighth grade is the football team."

"Are you the baseball coach?" Lonewolf asked her.

"Yep, I am."

He gave her a shy smile as we went through the gym doors.

In the packed cafeteria I wove my way through the hot-food line. I saw Russell over in the junk-food line. I sat down at a table with some other seventh-graders. In a few seconds Russell plopped three packages of Ding Dongs, a carton of milk, and a bag of potato chips on the table and sat down across from me. "History's sure a drag, isn't it?" he said.

I nodded and went on eating.

Russell's treacherous. He always acts real friendly to me and then when I don't expect it, he blurts out something about my dad in front of other kids. I don't know if it's because he's too dumb to know how I feel or if he can't resist showing off.

Unfortunately when I got to my last class of the day, he was in that one too. It was English, and I was tired and had that stuffy feeling from being cooped up too long. I found a seat as far away from Russell as I could.

I was looking out the window at the sunshine and wishing I were riding my bike to the river when I heard some kid burst out, "Well, aw right!"

I looked up to see Ms. Castle coming in the door. She dumped her books and papers on the teacher's desk, picked up a stack of small folded cards, and turned to give us a big smile. "You seem like a lively class. We should have a great year together."

All the kids, including me, smiled back at her.

"I'm an idiot about names. Can you save these cards and put them on your desk until I memorize your names? You can give me a test on Friday." She walked around the room, finding bodies to match her cards and looking carefully into each kid's face. I was nervous when she came up to me, took a second glance at the card, and then stared into my plain brown eyes. Her eyes were amber-colored with little green specks and they were fringed with thick, curly lashes.

"Gerald Johnson, Junior. Hmm," she murmured. "You look like a J.J. That's it. J.J."

She went on to the guy two seats in front of me. Each time she leaned over, she held her long auburn hair away from her face with her left hand. The hair cascaded down below her slim waist to her bottom, and I hid a grin behind my fingers as an impulse to smack that round rump passed through my mind.

"I think I'll have you write a partial autobiography this week," Ms. Castle told us when she'd finished passing out the name cards. "You can write about something funny or sad or unforgettable that happened to you. That way I'll get to know you a little better and have some idea of the grammar and punctuation we need to work on.

"First I'll read you some examples of other students' writing that might help you get started." She hitched herself up onto the front of her desk, opened a folder she'd taken off a pile of books, and began to read with her legs swinging in front of her.

It was a story by Mike Knight about a little kid's first day at school. It was pretty funny. The kid got caught cheating at seven-up and had to stand in the hall; he was

22

late coming in after recess because some third-graders chased him up a tree; somebody stepped on his lunch bag, so all he had for lunch were radishes, and he sat next to another kid who was so scared to ask to go to the bathroom that he wet his pants.

The class laughed. I laughed, too, but mostly I was eyeing Ms. Castle's arms and legs. Instead of her flesh gradually slimming toward her hands and feet, it plumped straight down until it ended in a crease at her wrist and ankles, like the arms and legs of a little kid's baby doll.

Ms. Castle turned to another page in her folder. "Now I'll read you one of my favorites, by Sue Anne Torres. It's sad, but as you've found out by now, not every Friday night is party time."

The story was about a six-year-old girl's parents getting a divorce. The story ended with the dad breaking his promise to visit the little girl. " 'I hate Daddy now.' " Ms. Castle made her voice sound like a sad six-year-old. " 'Anyway Mommy said we're going to have a new one. I wonder if he'll like me.' "

Just what I needed to hear at the end of the day.

Ms. Castle closed the folder. "I hope this gives all of you some idea of what a partial autobiography could be like. Don't worry about having the first draft perfect. We'll work on it all week. Tonight think over your life and pick out one sad, frightening, or funny event that you can start writing about in class tomorrow.

"There's the bell." She flashed us a big smile. "Good-bye!"

I picked up my books and walked slowly out the door toward my hall locker. There'd been plenty of sad and

23

frightening things in my life, but not any I wanted a teacher to know about.

I got off the school bus before Grace did and stood on the sidewalk waiting for her. It was plain she was dragging her tail even while she was hopping down the steps. "So, you had a good day at school," I said to her as we started down the street.

"Of course I did. On the way to fifth period two ninth-grade girls bumped me in the hall and one of them said, 'Yo, country girl, who dressed you?' "

"Well, if that's all that happened—"

"And in home ec the kids around me grabbed each other quick so they wouldn't get stuck with me. Then two jerks shoved a nerdy kid at me so he'd have to be my partner."

"Why didn't you just laugh it off?"

"Laugh it off!" Grace stopped in the middle of crossing the road. "Look at you. You can wear anything you want. You wore that sleeveless T-shirt to show off your muscles to Summer."

"What are you talking about?"

A car honked at us. We moved onto the curb and I was ready to drop the discussion, but Grace went on. "I'm talking about you just *happening* to sit behind Summer."

"Oh, and you *happened* to sit behind Clayton?"

"That was because I wanted to be by kids I know," Grace said primly.

"Come off it, PK." I call her PK whenever she acts like the preacher's kid she is.

We reached her house and she went inside to fight with her mother about her clothes. I picked up the mail, then went into my house to read a letter from my dad and wonder what I was going to use for an autobiography.

24

4

Losing It

The next morning Grace slammed out of her house and stomped down her front steps again. She was wearing another dorky outfit. This time it was a dress with a fancy lace collar. At the bus stop she turned the collar under, took a belt out of her purse, and tried to hitch up the dress. "Is this any better?" she asked.

"Sure," I said. Actually she looked like a lumpy pillow. She must have figured that out because she kept trying to pat the dress flat as the bus came up the road.

"Why don't you just wear jeans?" I wondered.

"Where do your last year's jeans come? To your knees?" she snapped. I got on the bus and took a seat across the aisle from her so I wouldn't have to listen to her moan about her clothes.

When I walked into history class, she was already at her desk with her sleeves rolled up. I said hi to Lonewolf as I passed him on the way to my seat. Summer came into the room right after me. She was wearing a purple tank top under a navy-blue vest. And shorts again. I was glad

25

Grace sat behind me. It'd be depressing to watch her watching Summer.

Clayton barely made it into his seat before the bell rang. Mrs. Beasley was already in front of the room with her green grade book poised in front of her face. After she took roll, she began a long sermon about the benefits the United States received from brave Captain Clark's journey to the West and how Sacagawea's invaluable guidance helped him through trials with the Indians.

I kept thinking that Sacagawea was an Indian. What was she doing helping a white man? I didn't think it would be smart to ask Beasley that question, though.

Clayton's brainy when it comes to books, but not when it comes to people. He raised his hand right in the middle of Mrs. Beasley's telling us how Sacagawea got horses from the Shoshones.

When Beasley called on him, he said, "Didn't Sacagawea harm her own people's future by getting them to give horses to the Lewis and Clark expedition?"

"I've explained to you that Sacagawea's husband, Toussaint Charboneau, was hired by Captain Clark as a guide. And that Captain Clark welcomed Sacagawea on the trip because her father was a Shoshone chieftain who had horses the expedition needed to travel through the mountains."

"Yes, but you also said the expedition paved the way for the white man to settle the Northwest," Clayton explained, "and didn't that help to wipe out the Indians?"

Mrs. Beasley frowned impatiently at Clayton. "That was hardly the point of Captain Clark's journey."

About then I was wondering what Lonewolf felt about all this. His head was tilted down and he seemed to be studying his hands, which were lying across his history book. Russell gave him a poke in the shoulder. "Hey, you're an Indian. What do you think?"

Mrs. Beasley smiled sweetly at Lonewolf. "Would you like to contribute something to our discussion, John?"

Lonewolf raised his head slowly and spoke so softly we had to strain our ears to hear. "My father said it would never be written in the history books that the white men slaughtered all the buffalo the Indians used for food and then tried to slaughter all the starving Indians."

The sugary smile faded from Mrs. Beasley's face as she stroked her neck with her fingers. "I don't know if I'd use the word *slaughter.*"

"Why not?" Clayton asked. "That's what we did."

"Will you please raise your hand before you talk!" Beasley's voice cracked like a whip against Clayton's face.

That shut him up. That shut us all up. Mrs. Beasley assigned us chapter two and we read quietly until the bell rang and she dismissed us with a wave of her arm.

At lunchtime Russell plunked his junk food on the table beside me. "Old Buffalo Butt sure lost it today," he said.

I nodded and swallowed half my sandwich whole so I could split the cafeteria without him. He caught up with me on the way to English, though. "You figured out what you're going to write for Castle?"

"Probably something about my mom's divorce," I said, barely turning my head toward him. I was going at a fast clip, but he kept on my tail.

"She dumped your old man, huh?"

I gave him another quick nod, went through the classroom door, and headed for my seat. Out of the corner of my eye I saw him hesitate and then move over to his side

27

of the room. The last person I wanted to talk to about my parents was Russell. He'd been there with Pete and Summer when the police took my dad away in handcuffs. And he was the one who had spread it around the school.

Ms. Castle came in, all shiny-faced and happy. "Everyone ready to go? Everyone picked out an event to write about?"

Nobody admitted they hadn't.

I decided to tell how my dad got canned from a job. How he'd be playing pool in the tavern and forget what time it was and then sleep through the alarm the next day. And how my mom blamed me for the divorce, because she was afraid I might turn out like my dad if she let him stay around me.

I didn't write anything about my dad going to prison. Ms. Castle collected our papers just before the bell rang. She said she'd save them so we could work on them some more.

On the way home from school Grace stumbled along beside me in her clodhopper brown oxfords. I tried to stay on neutral ground by talking about the crummy way Mrs. Beasley taught compared with Ms. Castle. I got a little carried away in describing how cool I thought Ms. Castle looked.

Grace eyed me with disgust. "I've seen Ms. Castle. She has fat arms."

"She isn't fat!"

"I didn't say she was fat. I said she has fat arms."

"Big deal."

"You're the one making the big deal out of it," Grace said. "Who cares if she has 'amber eyes and auburn hair.' You mean yellow eyes and red hair?"

"You know, PK, you used to be kinda fun to be around.

28

Now you're a big drag." I shouldn't have said that. It made her mouth droop again. I figured I'd better put up with hearing about what was making her miserable. "So. What happened in home ec today?"

She shrugged. "Nothing much."

We covered half a block before she started pouring it out. "Well, if you really want to know. We were supposed to practice making a pizza crust. I saw those two jerks, who are always making cracks about my clothes, hanging around my nerdy partner, Trevor, who was supposed to be mixing the flour and baking powder and salt. I rolled out the dough and stuck it in the oven.

"When Ms. Thornsbury came around to us for the taste test, she made a terrible face and spit our crust into a paper towel. She gave us an F and told us we should have measured our salt more carefully. All this time the two jerks were sitting on their stools with their heads on the counter so no one could see them laughing. As soon as Ms. Thornsbury moved to the side of the room, I went over and told them off."

That was the stupidest thing she could have done. Every time the guys got her to blow her top, they'd just plan something worse. But Grace was obviously in no mood for advice.

When we reached her house, we saw Matt in the driveway staring at his car. "You found it. Great!" I said before I realized the car was sitting on blocks. "Whoa, they ripped off your tires and wheels."

"And the stereo," Matt added sadly.

I walked around to the front of the car. "Did they get the engine?" Rattler, I remembered, was mainly interested in pulling engines.

"No," Matt said, "but an engine isn't going to do me much good without wheels."

"How are you going to get to the community college without a car?" Grace wondered. "Maybe Grandma will buy you new tires."

"She might, but she won't buy me a new stereo."

"Who found your car?" I asked.

"The cops, but I had to have it towed home."

Mrs. Elliott came out the front door. She was carrying a glass of pineapple juice for Matt. After she handed it to him, she turned to Grace. "How was school?"

"Just perfect, Mom. I was made fun of all day."

Mrs. Elliott frowned. "Oh, now—"

"She does look out of it, Mom," Matt said.

"She's almost in her teens," Mrs. Elliott told him. "And I think that dress is entirely appropriate."

"For Anne of Green Gables," Grace said.

I decided it was time to split for my house. I'd already spent enough years listening to Grace fight with her mother.

After I'd made myself a sandwich and grabbed a Pepsi out of the fridge, I settled down in the big chair in the living room. It was six months since my dad had been sent back up. And it must have been thirteen months since Rattler and Louis had been caught stealing a truck. Could they be out on parole so soon? I could find out by asking my dad, but I didn't feel much like writing to him.

I crushed the Pepsi can in my hand and started wondering if Ms. Castle would read our papers before she handed them back. I wondered what it would be like if I got sick and Ms. Castle came to see me and Mom and Willard were at the restaurant and there was nobody home but me. . . .

30

The phone rang. It was Mom wanting me to come to work because Willard had fired a busboy for yakking with the cooks instead of clearing tables. Working was okay with me. That would mean I'd have the money to go to the Locker Room in the mall and get some sweats for PE.

I didn't get home until after twelve and I was sleepy the next morning. When Grace started complaining about her plaid skirt, I told her to lighten up. I hadn't noticed Clayton or Summer putting her down.

"Clayton and Summer didn't put you down, either, when your dad went back to prison," she shot back. "And you were afraid to even show up at school."

"You've got things way out of proportion, PK," I told her.

I felt dopey through math and history, but PE woke me up. Ms. Kraft let us play a game against Pete's team. Lonewolf put Pete out by catching the ball he'd popped up behind home plate. And the next time Pete was up, I tagged him sliding into first base. That made my morning.

I saw Pete in the showers. He was under the showerhead nearest the wall. The way he kinda crouched with his back to the room made me wonder if he was ashamed of his body or was bummed out about losing the game.

I was still thinking about him when I was over by my locker pulling on my jeans. Three guys were sitting on a bench laughing about a gag Jenson and Taylor had pulled in home ec second period. After a girl put her cookies in an oven to bake, Taylor had walked by and switched her oven to Broil. The guys split their guts

remembering how she'd screamed when she opened the
oven and smoke poured out.

I thought it was funny, too, until I heard them call the
girl "Holy Grace."

5

Warm Bones

Mr. Wampler yelled at me in shop class. He was showing us how to use the table saw and I barely missed cutting my thumb off along with the hunk of board. This sent him into a tirade on how seventh-graders think they're too big to follow directions. How would he know what seventh-graders think?

The truth is I'm usually coordinated, but I was worrying about Grace being called "Holy Grace." If that name stuck, she was doomed in junior high.

When Wampler wound down, he told me to stand behind the other kids and to *pay attention.* I stood there the rest of the hour watching his big belly crease against the edge of the table while he bent over to position each kid's fingers on the boards as if we were all morons. After shop class was over, I stopped in the can to take a leak. Getting yelled at makes me nervous. And also I wanted to comb my hair before I went into Ms. Castle's room.

While Ms. Castle was passing out our autobiographies, she explained that there were no grades on them. Instead she'd put red lines under the sentences we

33

needed to work on. After we read our papers over, we could ask questions on anything we didn't understand before we began our revisions. That way each of us would have an opportunity to earn an A if we wanted to work hard. Believe me, in her class I wanted an A.

I noticed as she passed out the papers, she made soft comments to some of the kids. I sat there waiting for her to come up my aisle, wondering if she'd say anything to me. She did. "You've had quite a life, J.J.," she said.

I shrugged. Like it was no big deal. But being called "J.J." by her made my bones warm. It was as if I wasn't just Jerry Junior, the convict's kid, but a separate person from my dad.

The class fell silent while we pored over our papers. Then one kid after another raised a hand. She explained about adverbs at least four times and never got mad or chewed out the fourth kid for not listening. By the time most of the questions had been asked, I knew how to fix all my red lines. I gave Ms. Castle a big smile as I left the room. What a neat teacher.

I'd almost forgotten about Grace when I climbed on the bus and saw her sitting alone, staring out the window. I could tell how bummed she was by the way her forehead hung against the glass. I sat down beside her and dumped my math and English books on the floor in front of my feet. "Rough day, huh?"

She didn't turn her head. "I don't want to talk about it."

This time I knew she really didn't. I figured maybe my being around might help a little. After we got off the bus, we walked silently home. "See ya tomorrow," I said.

She just nodded and dragged her feet up to her porch.

I went in my house, got a Pepsi out of the fridge, took

my paper out of my English book, and settled down at the kitchen table to do my revision. I got all the *ly*s on my adverbs and was starting on commas when I gave up and threw my pen across the room.

I had to do something about Grace. We used to play basketball after school in my backyard, and go biking, and she was a blast, except when she acted like her mother and pulled the goody-goody routine. And that wasn't too often. Mostly when I was still ripping things off and she didn't want any part of it.

Now she moped around in her dorky clothes and screamed at Jenson and Taylor instead of laughing off their gags. Last year she would have done them one better, but last year she looked like all the other kids in her jeans and shirts. It was stupid to have clothes matter so much. And I was going to feel even stupider trying to explain all this to the Reverend. I downed the last of the Pepsi, crunched the can, and took off.

I cut behind my garage and the Elliotts' garage to get to the church, which is on the corner. I walked through the back hall and knocked on the Reverend's office door, half hoping that he wasn't there. He was. "Hello, Jerry," he said. "Come on in."

There was a pile of papers on his desk, but he ignored them and dropped his huge body into one of the leather chairs by the window. That guy must be at least six feet four. The ends of his long black mustache come to the bottom of his chin. He stroked the mustache while I settled down in the chair beside him.

I searched around in my head for a way to get started, stared at my feet a bit, and then looked up at Reverend Elliott, figuring I'd just plunge in. But nothing came out of my mouth.

35

"Ah, how are things going along with your stepfather?" the Reverend asked me.

"Okay, I guess." What was there to say about stingy old Willard?

"Heard from your dad?"

"I got a letter a couple days ago. He's going to learn landscaping. He thinks maybe an outdoor job will help him stay straight when he gets released again."

The Reverend nodded. "That might keep him away from temptation."

I noted the *might*. I don't think the Reverend has much faith in my dad. A three-time loser is a hard guy to have faith in.

I concentrated on the knots in my shoelaces. "Um, I don't really have any bad problems right now, but Grace does."

"What's happening with Grace?"

So I tried to tell him about her trouble in home ec. It didn't sound like a big deal. When I'd finished, the Reverend said, "Perhaps I'd better talk with Grace. She seems to be making her relationships with the other students worse by taking everything too seriously."

"I've already told her that," I explained. "It's too late for a little talk. You see, the guys have already tagged her. She's embarrassed about how she looks and she gets defensive and acts like her mom, so they call her 'Holy Grace.' " Oops. I shot a glance at the Reverend. I hadn't meant to put down his wife.

He patted my shoulder. "I think I understand now."

I got up to go. "Maybe you could buy her some regular clothes and then she'd feel better and then it'd be easier for her to act like her old self."

36

He stood up too. "That's a possibility. Thank you very much for coming in, Jerry."

"That's okay," I said, and got out of there.

After I'd eaten my dinner and written my autobiography over in my neatest handwriting, I went out in the dark and climbed up to my tree house. The fight had already begun. I could hear Mrs. Elliott yelling something about Grace and a church school and then Grace screeching and then the low rumble of the Reverend's deep voice. Their kitchen blinds were closed, so I couldn't see what was going on. It got too cold for me to sit outside. I went back in the house and watched TV until I was sleepy enough to go to bed.

I don't say prayers, but that night I wished the Reverend would come through for Grace. Twice Grace had gotten him to save my butt. I'd hardly thanked her for it. Just called her a bigmouth.

And that's what she called me when she knocked on my door the morning after I talked to the Reverend about her. She was grinning, though, just like I'd been.

"Quick, bigmouth, let me come in. I want to borrow some of your clothes."

I opened the door wider, trying to focus on what she'd said. I hadn't even finished my breakfast and wasn't quite awake. "My clothes?"

"Ya, let's check out your closet."

I followed her into my room. "We have to be quiet. Mom and Willard are still sleeping."

"This won't make any noise." She opened my closet door and began flipping through the hangers. "Gol, you've got a department store in here. You must put everything you make on your back."

"I like to look good."

37

"Ha, and you're the one who tells me to lighten up about the trash Mom buys me." She pulled out a yellow sweater, held it up to her chest, and looked at herself in the mirror over my dresser. "Your colors are awful on me."

"What do you expect?" I asked. "You've got blue eyes and black hair and I've got brown eyes and brown hair."

"There must be something." She pawed through the hangers again. "Black, that's it. We can both wear black."

She took down my black T-shirt with green stripes on the sleeves. "Turn around. I'm going to put this thing on."

"I'll finish my breakfast."

I was running water into my bowl in the sink when she came into the kitchen. "Well, what do you think?" she asked.

The T-shirt was too big for her, but it looked pretty good slopped over her old jeans. When she caught me checking her pant legs, she stared down at the ragged bottoms. "Are the jeans all right? I spent half the night ripping out seams to make them longer."

"They beat your Bo-Peep outfits," I said. "Let's get moving."

It was raining outside. She stuffed her white blouse into the pocket of her slicker and we took off for the bus. "Since tomorrow's Saturday," she told me as we hurried along in the rain, "Dad's going to take me shopping at the mall."

"Can I go too? I need some sweats for PE."

"Sure. There's plenty of room in his car. Mom isn't coming."

"I bet. I heard her yelling."

"She wanted to send me to a church school where the

38

kids wear uniforms, but Dad said I needed to learn to get along in contemporary society. She wouldn't talk to me this morning after she saw me in these old pants, but I don't care."

Grace jumped on the bus, which had just drawn up to the curb, and I jumped on after her.

In history class Clayton gave her a second look as he came into the room. I turned my head to see if she noticed. She did. Summer turned, too, and told her she liked her top.

"Shhh, Beasley's coming," I said real quick. I didn't want Grace telling Summer it was my shirt and giving her the wrong idea about our relationship.

Beasley showed us a film about early logging in Washington State. I was watching two men in long johns pull a saw back and forth through a huge cedar tree and thinking I'd never be able to wear my new black T-shirt to school, when I noticed Summer jerk over to the side of her seat. She pulled a tissue out of her purse and wiped off the corner of her desk. When she wiped her desk off a second time, I peered through the darkened room at Russell.

Sure enough, his head was facing Summer and his lips were pouching in and out to gather saliva on his tongue. Before he could gleek again, I slipped out of my seat, crawled up beside his, and slugged him in the arm. "Summer doesn't like spit," I told him, and crawled back to my desk.

From the corner of my eye I could see Buffalo Butt craning her neck our way, but she didn't turn off the film.

When class was over, Summer whispered a thanks to me before she stuffed her purse into her book bag and left. Summer never sticks up for herself. I don't mind defending her, though I was a little uneasy about Russell taking revenge with his big mouth.

I ate lunch with Lonewolf and didn't see Russell again until I got to Ms. Castle's room. She collected our autobiographies and then had us open our English books to a play called *The Glass Menagerie*. About five guys raised their hand to be the brother, Tom. Jeff got to read the part first, then Russell next, and then me.

"Well, J.J.," she said when I finished, "you're a natural."

I've always been good at acting, but instead of walking out of that room when the bell rang, I felt like dancin'.

6

Big Mouth

Before I left with Grace and her dad Saturday afternoon, it was my turn to have a family fight. I didn't know Mom was taking the day off to spend time with me. She didn't know I'd planned to go to the mall, and was hurt that I didn't want to do something with her. Willard was pissed because neither one of us was going to work in his restaurant.

Mom sat in the big chair with her head bowed and her fingers curled against her lips. I stood in the middle of the room wondering whether to go or stay while Willard shot his mouth off. He couldn't understand why I needed more clothes, since I already dressed better than he did. He said that I should learn to work hard and save my money so I wouldn't expect to get something for nothing like my father.

That did it. The Reverend honked his car horn and I split.

On the way to the mall Grace bounced around in the front seat, gabbing to her dad about the clothes she wanted to buy. I sat in the backseat relieved that I didn't have to contribute to the conversation. It took all my energy to fight down the guilt I felt about leaving Mom alone. Willard only closed the restaurant Sundays after brunch. In the six months Mom had been married to Willard, she hadn't taken more than ten days off. Willard claimed renting was like poking money down a rat hole, and he wanted to save for a down payment on a house. I could see why Mom went along with this. After all, the only solid thing she'd had from my dad was a car, and I'd always wondered how he'd gotten that.

The Reverend parked his Toyota in front of Nordstrom. "Listen," Grace said to me as we walked toward the store, "it'll take me longer to buy my stuff than it will take you to get yours. Why don't you meet us at the Brass Plum when you're done?"

So, while Grace and the Reverend rode up the escalator, I wove myself through Nordstrom's perfume and jewelry counters and out into the mall corridors to the shop called the Locker Room. A zit-faced salesman tried to push Day-Glo orange sweats on me, telling me that was what "all the guys were wearing." I bought the dark brown ones that had a red streak of lightning across the back. Just enough. Just right.

I took my time getting back to Grace. I wandered through a shop called From the Waist Up. It had some neat stuff, but I was down to three dollars. I bought a chocolate chip cookie at the Cookie Stand and munched it while I made my way up Nordstrom's escalator and over to the Brass Plum.

The first thing that hits you when you reach that section of the store is the rock music. They must have ten speakers and ten TVs hanging from the posts between the racks of clothes, which are packed so close you might as well be in a jungle. I finally came upon the Reverend sitting in a chair by the dressing rooms, stroking his mustache.

I dropped into the seat next to him. "Having fun?"

"I think Grace is," he said.

She whisked out of the hall, leaned over our chairs, and asked, "How do I look?"

"Your mother's going to puke," I said.

"But how do I look?"

"Good." She did. She was wearing black jeans, a light blue crew under a navy denim shirt dotted with swirls of pink, purple, and green. And over that she wore a black leather vest. The whole thing wasn't that far out. It was just that I didn't think her mom would be able to swallow black leather.

The Reverend didn't blink, though. "If that's what you want" is all he said.

Grace wore her outfit home. She got the Reverend to buy us sundaes on the way. When we reached her house, she invited me in for a game of chess, but I didn't care to be around when Mrs. Elliott saw her preacher's daughter.

Mom had roast chicken and mashed potatoes waiting for me. We sat down to dinner smiling at each other. It was like the old days. My dad has been in and out of prison since I was nine, and until Willard came along, Mom and I'd spent most of that time together.

While I made a hollow in my potatoes for the butter to swim in, I told Mom about Ms. Castle. About how she tried to help all the students succeed and that she said I was a natural actor.

Mom nodded. "Your dad was a pretty good actor too."

"Ya, but I think I'll make it straight," I told her.

"That'd be nice," she agreed. "And it'd also be nice if you visited your father."

"How come? He never wanted me to see him in prison before?"

She placed her fork on the side of her plate, tilted her head, and gave me a thoughtful look. "How long has it been since you've written him?"

"I don't know. A couple of weeks, I guess."

"More than a couple of weeks," she said.

"Maybe." I took a gulp of my milk. "School's going on, you know."

She took a drink of her coffee. "I know. And I know that as you get older, you get involved in interests other than your family."

"Willard's not much of a family, Mom."

"I understand that's how it seems. But you have to understand Willard. He grew up sleeping on a couch in his grandmother's apartment. And he wants his own home now. For all of us. And these days it takes a large down payment to get one."

I finished the last of my chicken and wiped my mouth on my paper napkin before I told her, "He's making a slave of you."

"No, he isn't. I want our own home too."

"Anyway he isn't much of a dad."

She shrugged. "I don't expect that will ever be easy for him. He never knew his father and he's never had any children. But you have your own dad. How about going to see him a week from tomorrow?"

"I'll write him a letter tonight." I got up to leave the table.

She got up, too, and put her hand on my shoulder. "Wait a minute. We have pie. Let's have it à la mode."

44

I sat back down and waited for her to serve the dessert. I didn't much want to see my dad. I've always been scared of prisons. When I was little, Mom used to drive me to Monroe to get my clothes at a church shop for prisoners' families. I always kept my eyes on the dashboard when we were on the road below the reformatory. I was afraid of catching sight of the walls and the big towers that sat up on the hill.

Mom didn't say anything more until I was almost finished with my pie. And then she said, "Jerry, your dad really needs a visit from you."

"Did he write you a letter?" I asked.

"No, he phoned. He worries that you never forgave him for getting caught stealing in front of your friends."

"Well, it wasn't a picnic," I said. "Anyway I wrote him last spring that it was okay. Some kids still talk to me."

Mom leaned across the table. "That isn't enough for him now. He needs to see you and hug you and know he's still your dad."

"What is this?" I asked. "You were always afraid I'd get contaminated by him."

"You're older now," she said. "And you're all he's got."

I pushed my plate away. "Do I have a choice?"

"I don't think so," she said. "I'll take you up there a week from tomorrow. On Sunday afternoon."

The next night I had a dream about my dad and Ms. Castle. She came into an appliance store where Dad was a salesman. I was sitting on the edge of the bookkeeper's desk waiting for Dad to finish his shift. Ms. Castle caught sight of me and walked toward the desk.

45

From the corner of my eye I checked out Dad. He was waiting on an old, white-haired lady. As he bent down to show her the insides of a refrigerator, I saw that he was wearing overalls with the words *Monroe Reformatory* stitched on the back.

I said hello to Ms. Castle, slid off the desk, and put my hand on her shoulder to walk her away from Dad. The material of her coat was soft under my hand, and I felt proud that I was taller than she was and could look down at her as I steered her toward the ovens. I was pointing to the glass door on the front of a microwave when Dad moved in between us and threw his arm around me.

"I see you know my boy," he said to Ms. Castle.

"Oh, yes," she said. "J.J. is one of my favorite students."

"J.J.?" Dad's face fell. His arm dropped to his side. And I woke up.

It took me a long time to go to sleep after that dream. I kept remembering the pictures in Mom's photo album. Especially the one where I'm about two and riding on Dad's shoulders and Dad has a big pumpkin grin on his face. He named me after him because, he says, I'm the son he always wanted. He writes me every week. He writes letters that are filled with hope that the next time he gets out, he'll make up for everything he's done in the past. The same promises that he's broken before.

I tried to go to sleep on my back, on my side, and then on my stomach. The trouble was that even though I knew he loved me, I thought my life would be easier without him.

When I pulled myself out of bed in the morning, I felt heavy-eyed and crabby. On the way to school Grace skipped along beside me light as a feather. "What did your mom say?" I asked her.

"Nothing. She still isn't speaking to me," Grace said, and leapt for the steps of the bus.

By history class I was awake. Summer told Grace that her outfit was great. Clayton twisted around in his seat, looked Grace over, and said, "That shirt makes your eyes even bluer."

Grace turned pink.

Beasley came into the room swabbing her eyes with a wad of Kleenex. At first I thought she was crying, but when she sneezed twice and mopped up her mouth and nose, I figured she must have a cold. She evidently wasn't up to a lecture on the natural resources of the Northwest, because she told us to read chapter five in our books and she'd give us a quiz on Friday.

While Beasley crouched over her desk, sneezing and coughing and pulling out tissues from her Kleenex box, we read about salmon spawning in Washington State. Or most of the kids did. For a while I stared at the map on page sixty-seven, which showed how the salmon traveled up the rivers from Puget Sound, and then I got distracted by Summer's neck.

Two tendons run up the back of her neck under her white skin. There's a hollow between the tendons that I wanted to touch. She reminds me of the crippled sister in *The Glass Menagerie.* Not that Summer's crippled, but that she's almost too gentle to believe. Summer has short yellow hair that curls in tufts like a baby duck's feathers. It would feel soft as down slipping through my fingers.

Beasley let out a huge "Haah-choo" that sent the kids in the front seats reeling back. "Excuse me. Excuse me,"

47

she said, snatching a dry batch of tissues from her box and plastering them over her face.

I noticed Russell wasn't concentrating on salmon either. He couldn't turn a page without sneaking a glance at Summer. Summer never looked his way unless he gleeked at her. Instead of trying to get attention by showing off, I thought he should ask for weights at Christmas and work off his flab, or he'd stay a "wannabe" forever.

Russell didn't bother me at lunch and he was in his seat again when I got to Castle's room. Ms. Castle was there, too, all fresh and pretty with three yellow roses pinned in the side of her long hair. Had someone given her the roses?

We finished the scenes from *The Glass Menagerie* that were in our English book, and then Ms. Castle passed out copies of a TV comedy. She said it was a satire on cops-and-robbers shows. I thought maybe it would be like the Max Smart play we did in sixth grade, but it wasn't. This one had superintelligent cops who conferred over prints of DNA and jock-type robbers who slapped each others' bottoms when they shot the cops in the forehead and brains poured out.

I had trouble deciding on the character I wanted to play. While I was trying to choose, Ms. Castle gave out the cop parts. The girls got more than half of them because, Ms. Castle said, this was the nineties.

I put up my hand for the bloodthirstiest robber. Six other kids did too.

"Choose Johnson for the part," Russell told Ms. Castle. "He's a natural to be a thief. He knows all about stealing."

"What do you mean?" Ms. Castle asked.

Russell jerked his head toward me. "Ask him."

My raised hand slowly sunk down to my sickened stomach, and the room was quiet as death.

7

Tryout

As soon as I heard Mom coming toward my door, I blew my nose on a hunk of toilet paper. "Jerry," she said, "what are you doing home? Are you sick?"

"I've got a terrible cold," I told her, keeping the toilet paper over my nose.

"Where did you get that? Let me feel your forehead." She placed her cool palm against my skin. "You don't seem to have a fever."

"It's my history teacher's fault. She sprayed germs all over us."

"Well, maybe if you stay in bed today, you'll feel well enough to go to school tomorrow."

I doubted that, but I rested my head back on my pillow in what I hoped was a limp, sickly manner.

"I'll get you some vitamin C and something to drink. You need to take in lots of fluids." She didn't close my door behind her and she was back in no time with a couple of white pills and a glass of orange juice.

I lifted my head off the pillow, swallowed the pills, and sipped at the juice.

"Would you like me to stay home with you today?" she asked.

"No, no. That's okay. I'm just tired from coughing all night."

She went to get Willard's breakfast, or more like lunch, since they don't get up until ten thirty. She brought me a tray with oatmeal and more orange juice before she left for the restaurant. As soon as I heard the car pull out of the garage, I put the tray on the table beside my bed and threw off my covers.

I thought I'd feel better after a shower, but instead I sank down on the living room couch feeling as sick as I'd acted. I knew I'd brought everything on myself by punching Russell when he was trying to get Summer's attention. It was a stupid move. Big hero, Johnson. Now what?

There wasn't anything to say to Ms. Castle. Any excuse. Any explanation for Russell's attack. I was just as tongue-tied now as when Russell told her I knew all about stealing.

I lay on that couch most of the afternoon wondering if Willard would give me a permanent job in the restaurant, wondering if Mom would let me quit school, and all the time knowing they wouldn't. About a quarter to four Grace banged on my front door.

"You don't look sick to me," she said after I let her in. "When you called me last night, I thought you must be dying."

"I am dying," I told her, "and I didn't want you knocking at my door this morning waking up Mom."

"Well, you may be dying, but you're obviously not sick." She plopped herself down in the big chair, holding my black T-shirt in her lap.

I stretched out on the davenport.

"So?" she asked. "What's your sad story?"

"Ms. Castle probably thinks I'm a thief."

"Just because of what Russell said? Everybody knows Russell's a bigmouth."

"And half the school knows my dad's been sent up."

"Listen, Jerry, people know it. It's a fact, but your mom's married to a restaurant owner now. You've got a new stepdad. You're in the clear."

I gave up arguing with her. She didn't get the point. I wanted to be J.J., the natural actor. I didn't want Ms. Castle to think of me as low-class. But if I tried to explain this to Grace, she'd just say I was hung up on Suzy Castle. And I was hung up on what Suzy Castle thought. I wanted Grace to leave.

"I think I'll go to sleep for a while," I told her.

"And you called me a drag." She held out my T-shirt. "Here. I brought this back."

"You can keep it," I said.

"I washed it. It's all clean."

"I know, but I don't need it."

"Gol, thanks." She hesitated at the front door. "I hope you're well tomorrow."

"Maybe," I said, "but don't come over in the morning."

The next morning Mom put her foot down and said I'd absolutely have to go to the doctor if I wasn't well by Thursday. Thursday I chose school. What else?

I hung around Lonewolf in PE. Somehow he always makes me feel better. In history Summer asked me if I'd had the flu. "No," I said, "just a bad cold."

In Castle's room I slipped into my seat as the bell rang.

I guess the kids had performed the satire on Friday because she assigned another paper. It was to be about a conversation at midnight. While she went over the punctuation rules for dialogue, I concentrated on the pencil marks on my desk. I didn't want her looking at me or calling on me.

She gave us class time to start our paper. At first the only conversations at midnight I could think of were fights between my mom and dad, but twenty minutes before the class was over, I hit upon the idea of writing about the night Matt's car was stolen. And maybe, if I did that, Ms. Castle would think that's how I knew about thieves.

I was pouring the memory of the night on paper as fast as I could, when Ms. Castle stopped by my desk. "Here's your autobiography, J.J. You did a nice job."

I looked quickly at the paper she'd given me. Three spelling mistakes. B-plus. I didn't look at her. Just mumbled, "Thanks."

Before the period ended, Ms. Castle announced that the drama club was going to produce a school play, and tryouts would be held the next day after school. She wanted to encourage all of us to try out for a part. "You especially, J.J.," she said.

I had to work at the restaurant that evening, but whenever I had time by myself, I wrestled with the problem of the tryouts. Sometimes I decided I would go and sometimes I decided I wouldn't. Pete and I had been cast in a play in sixth grade, but when Pete's mom found out about my dad, she yanked him out of the play and had him transferred into another classroom. It was just as well, because Pete was staying two yards away from me when we rehearsed a scene together.

I was still going "Yes, no, yes, no" when Ms. Castle called after me as I left her room the next day. "See you in the auditorium, J.J."

Three of the front rows in the auditorium were filled with kids when I got there. I took a place on the aisle in the fifth row. Ms. Castle was on stage helping two ninth-graders set up a cart that held a VCR and a camcorder. After the wires were plugged in, she came to the front of the stage.

"I'm delighted that so many of you turned out," she said in a voice that carried to the back of the hall. "The name of the play we're doing is *The Bad Seed*. It is about a young girl who has no conscience and will stop at nothing to get her way or to take revenge.

"These tryouts will be held like a professional casting. There is a chalk line on the stage that you are expected to stand behind. Be aware of the line with your peripheral vision. Do not look down at your feet. Before you begin your reading, say your name and your homeroom number. Talk slowly and distinctly, always acting as if you're happy to be here.

"Each of you will be reading a part cold, but take a minute to look over the page. Hold the script up high when you are speaking so your face is toward the camera. Keep your place with your thumb, not your finger. Pretend you are talking to another person. Be animated if the part calls for it. Hear your voice go up and down."

At this point Ms. Castle read some lines that were supposed to be spoken by a woman asking advice from a mystery writer. At first Ms. Castle read the part in a droning voice. Next she talked excitedly, as if she really wanted to know about mysteries.

It'd be a cinch for me to make lines believable, I

thought. I'd had plenty of practice watching my dad con people.

Ms. Castle started with the first girl in the front row. She was a big, lanky ninth-grade thing and she read in a droning voice just like Ms. Castle had told her not to do. Ms. Castle kept the camcorder on her until she was finished, then she thanked the girl and asked for the next student. He was a seventh-grader, a new friend of Pete's. He couldn't read very well and kept stumbling over the words. Halfway through he asked Ms. Castle if he could start again.

"Never stop in a tryout," she told him. "Even if you make a mistake, just pull yourself together and keep right on going."

He did a little better toward the finish. But not much. Ms. Castle thanked him and said, "Next."

That was Pete. I slid down in my seat as I watched his tryout. He was good. Pete's almost as good as I am. And he knows it too. He had a grin on his face as he bounced off the stage, but when he caught sight of me, his face went blank.

I watched him sit back down. He said something to the guy beside him. The guy turned around and took a quick look at me. It didn't take any imagination to know what Pete had told him.

I waited until Ms. Castle had her camera focused on another ninth-grade girl. Then I got up and split out of the auditorium.

8

Convict's Kid

I woke up early Sunday and stared out the window. The rain was drizzling into the fir tree, leaving fat drops of water on the ends of its needles. Six thirty. Four hours to go until Mom got up and three more hours until we left to visit Dad.

My stomach was already crunching, and I knew before the day was over, it'd be feeling worse. There wasn't a chance of going back to sleep. I pulled on my clothes and went out on the porch to get the paper.

Reading the funnies and sports page wasted forty-five minutes. Grace goes to church Sunday morning, so I couldn't bike-ride with her. I didn't feel like riding alone or listening to the Reverend preach. I turned on the TV and wasted two hours watching dumb cartoons.

Mom made pancakes, which was a bust because Willard wanted to hurry down to the restaurant and I couldn't eat. I watched baseball on Channel 11 until one o'clock and Mom was saying, "Come on, Jerry. I don't want to be late. It will make your dad anxious."

I didn't look at the towers on the hill when we rode

along the road below the reformatory. I clutched my stomach and said over and over to myself that in a couple of hours the visit would be done and I'd be going back home. Mom parked the car and I took a quick glance at the building beside us. It looked just like any other big office building.

"Is this where he meets us?" I asked.

"No. No," she said. "This is the administration. We have to go through here to get to the prison."

The word *prison* clanked in my head. "Mom, I don't know if I can go in."

"Jerry, he's waiting for you."

"But I think it will make me sick."

"Honey, you've known all along that he's in prison."

"Yes, but seeing him there is different."

She thought a minute, looking down at her lap, then shook her head. "I simply can't tell him that you're out in the car and won't come in. He'd be so hurt." She gathered up her purse and keys, leaned over and opened my door, and gave me a little shove. "Let's go."

I kept gulping for air on the way up the steps and into the building. Mom showed her picture ID at the reception desk. We climbed the stairs to the second floor and went through a metal scanner there. It looked just like the ones at the airport, only it felt creepier. What did the guard standing over us expect us to have? Guns? Knives?

He stamped my hand and Mom's hand and nodded to another guard in a glass enclosure. That one must have pushed a button, because a door in the back wall opened. I followed Mom through. The door shut behind us, leaving us alone in a hall that was about fifty feet long. "I'm scared," I said.

"It's all right." She took my hand. While our footsteps

echoed against the walls, I held on so tight the sweat squished between our palms.

At the end of the long hall there was another door and beside it another glassed-in control booth. The guard in there watched us until we were about three feet away. Then he must have pressed a button, because the door swung wide.

Inside was a big room with some people sitting around tables. Four little kids were on the floor in front of a TV. The kids were squealing over the video game two of them were playing.

Mom pushed me forward and I heard the door shut behind us. Out of the corner of my eye I saw a man spring up from a table. It was Dad. He crossed that room and had me by the shoulders in about two seconds. "My boy," he said. "My boy!"

He held me away from him and looked into my face and I looked into his. There were lines running down from his nose to his mouth that hadn't been there before. And his hair was thinner.

"You're getting so big," he said. "You're almost as big as I am. Oh, my boy."

He hugged me to him and I could feel him tremble. When he let me go, he blinked his eyes fast, then held out a hand to Mom. "Hello, Lily. You look as beautiful as ever."

Mom shook his hand and nodded. She is a pretty mom. Blond hair and big brown eyes.

"Come on. Come on. Let's sit down." Dad urged us toward a table. "Would you like some coffee, Lily? How about a Coke, Jerry?"

"Okay," I said.

There were vending machines along the back wall beside the TVs. I helped Dad carry two coffees and a Coke back to the table. "No sugar and a spot of cream," he said to Mom as he handed her a cup.

She returned his smile, but hers was a distant, cool smile, reminding him that she was just there to bring me. I saw this register in Dad's eyes and his shoulders straighten.

A guard in blue pants and shirt passed by our table. There were two others walking around the back of the room. They acted like the president's Secret Service men you see on TV, swiveling their heads this way and that. I jabbed my thumb toward the one who'd just passed us. "Those guys carry guns?"

"No," Dad said. "They just keep eye contact and watch to be sure the rules are observed and no contraband is passed."

"You mean like drugs?" I asked.

"Sometimes." Dad put his hand on my arm. "How's school?"

"It's okay. I've got one neat teacher, one nice teacher, one fair teacher, and two dorks."

"Is the neat one pretty?" he asked.

"Ya, real pretty." I gave him my gap-toothed grin and he returned it with his gap-toothed grin. And for a moment I thought how great it had been having him around. We always knew what each other was thinking.

"And that blue-eyed girl next door," he said, "is she growing up?"

"The hard way," I told him.

"I remember that girl as a real butt kicker."

"She's not kicking many butts now. Junior high seems to have thrown her."

60

Dad drank the last of his coffee. "Yep, changes can throw you."

I thought I'd better drop that. "Well," I said after a couple minutes, "how're you doing?"

"Fine," he said. "Fine. I'm still landscaping. Turns out I'm pretty good at growing things. I shouldn't have any trouble getting a job in a nursery when I leave here."

"Sounds good," I said. Mom didn't say anything.

There was another silence at our table. The kids were still squealing over by the TVs. A bowlegged prisoner was standing behind them watching their game. He reminded me of Rattler.

"Say," I said, "what happened to Rattler?"

"He's doing time," Dad said.

"Are you sure he's still in?"

"Yeah, he got five years." Dad leaned close to me. "Why? What made you think of him?"

"Grace's brother's car got stolen. So I wondered what Rattler was doing. I was trying to figure out who knew Matt's car was always in the driveway."

"Anyone driving by casing the neighborhood would know." Dad stared into his empty coffee cup. The skin on his face had sagged into a sad, hunted look. He got up quickly, picked up the cups, and headed for the garbage can.

I sucked in a breath and snuck a glance at Mom. She was frowning at me. "Talk about cheerful things."

"You aren't helping much," I said. "You're just sitting there."

Someone behind us started to cry. I turned to see what was going on. A man and a woman and a kid about ten years old were huddled around a table. The woman had her head bowed, sobbing. The man was stroking the

61

back of her neck, trying to calm her down. The kid was watching them with a sick look on his face.

When I turned back around, I saw Dad cutting between the tables. He was bouncing on the balls of his feet and smiling. Anybody who didn't know him would think he was happy. He's a good actor.

"Come on," he said to me when he reached us. "I'll beat you at a video game."

"You wish." I got out of my chair and followed him over to a TV. We played five games. I laughed and joked and acted like I was having a great time, trying hard to make up for bumming him out.

When Mom came over to say it was time to go, I put the zapper on top of the TV. "You know they stamped our hands," I told Dad, "but they must have made a mistake because they were out of ink."

"They don't make mistakes," he said flatly. "It's invisible ink. You'll have to put your hand under that black light there before you leave."

I glanced around the room. "Where?"

"Right next to the door."

The light looked like a desk lamp stuck to the wall. "What's on my hand?"

"A figure. They use a different one every day. Security." He put his arm around me and walked me toward the door.

Mom said good-bye and hurried ahead to the lamp so the guard in the glass cage could check her hand. Dad slowed our walk. His arm tightened on my shoulder. "I hated to have you see me in here, Jerry, but I didn't want you to forget me."

"I won't forget you." I stopped to give him a quick hug, but he held on, trembling again, like he couldn't let me go. When he did, I was afraid he might cry. I mumbled good-bye fast, went up to have my hand checked, and followed Mom out the opened door.

Mom and I didn't talk while we walked down the long hall. Out in the car I slumped down in my seat. "Dad seems to think he can keep straight doing landscaping."

"So he says." She started up the engine.

I reached over and turned on the radio. Loud.

9

Way to Go

Grace and her mother were at it again in the morning. I could hear them when I reached the walkway going to their house. I watched the door open, heard Grace scream, "Can't you let me take care of it by myself?" and then watched her slam the door before she pounded down her steps.

She was wearing her leather vest and my black shirt under her slicker. "Your mom doesn't like my clothes," I said.

"She hates your clothes and my clothes, and she's going to school at four o'clock today to take all her hate out on my home-ec teacher." Grace yanked the slicker's hood over her head.

I had the collar turned up on my jacket, but the pouring rain was still going down my neck. I hunched my shoulders around my ears as we started down the street together. "Why's your mom after Thornsbury?"

"Because I got a poor-work slip."

"*You* got a poor-work slip?"

"I flunked two of the cooking tests, remember?"

65

"Why didn't you tell your mom you'd bring up your grade before report cards come out?"

"I did. But she wanted to know why, why, why I got a poor-work slip when I already knew how to cook. So I had to tell her."

I halted right in the middle of the sidewalk, letting the rain beat on my face. "You told her? You told on Jenson and Taylor? Talk about stupid!"

"What else could I do?"

She could have done anything else, anything at all. Anything but rat on Jenson and Taylor. They were just horsing around. She should have laughed at them.

But I couldn't say that. She was already puckered up to cry. She knew she'd done the dumbest thing she could have done. I think her mother messes up her brain.

The bus came sloshing down the street. "We better run for it," I said, grabbing Grace by her wet slicker. On the bus she took a seat beside another girl and I was glad. My visit to the reformatory had depressed me enough.

We had a math quiz first period and it kept my mind occupied for an hour. After that I was moseying down the hall thinking about my dad when I saw Summer coming toward me. I thought she'd turn to go into Beasley's room, but she didn't. She came straight up to me. "Jerry, what are you thinking about?"

"Not much," I said.

"You look so sad." Summer only comes up to my chin, and she had to tilt her head back to see into my face.

Summer's soft and fragile and curvy, and I was totally thrown. I managed what I hoped was a nonchalant smile, put my arm around her, and walked her toward Beasley's door. "Life's sad," I said, then took another look at her. "You've got circles under your eyes!"

"I know. The twins were sick in the night and I got up to take care of them."

"Weren't your parents home?"

"Yes, but they both worked late."

"The kids woke you up instead?"

"My little sister did. My little brother was throwing up in his bed."

"Ugh." I shuddered as we went through Beasley's door, and Summer laughed. I guess she didn't mind being mama.

Russell was already in his seat and he opened his book fast when he saw us come into the room together. It was all I could do to keep from slugging him as I passed his desk. Beasley waddled in with another film can. History teachers get to sit out every other day.

Through the first part of the film I watched salmon try to jump up a fish ladder, and the rest of the time I stared at the back of Summer's neck and thought how it would feel to run my fingers down it.

When class was over, Mrs. Beasley confronted Clayton. "Young man, I don't think an earring is the proper thing to wear to school."

Clayton dropped his eyelids to half-mast. "You're wearing them."

"Yes, but I'm a woman. I don't think they look masculine on a boy."

"Everyone's welcome to an opinion," he said, and left her standing there with her mouth open.

I don't know what Beasley would do if Clayton dyed his hair purple like he did in sixth grade. I asked him once what his parents thought about it and he said his parents considered it his own business since it was his own body.

67

I was laughing to myself about Clayton as I walked down a hall after lunch. I'd been to the math room checking on the quiz scores the teachers always post beside their doors. I got a C-plus. I'd looked at Clayton's class scores too. He got an A of course. My C-plus suited me fine, though, and I was still smiling when I came to the main hallway by the girls' bathroom.

The first thing I saw was Jenson and Taylor and a kid named Morgan filling balloons with water at the wall fountain. Somebody's going to get it, I thought, and eased to the side a bit. As I did, a couple of girls came out of the can. One of them was Grace. Wham! A balloon shot across the hall, hit the brick wall two inches from her head, and doused her with a quart of water.

Grace looked down at her splotched leather vest, let out a wail, and backed into the bathroom. Jenson and Taylor fell down laughing.

Clarice, a long, stringy thing in my PE and English classes, came walking out next. Morgan took aim, but before he could fire, Clarice zipped across the hall, snatched the balloon out of his hand, and squeezed it like a squirt gun. Jenson and Taylor crouched on the floor, covering their faces with their hands. Morgan tried to jump on Clarice's back. She whirled around and gave it to him in the eyes.

"Ratch!" somebody yelled.

We scattered like mice. Most of the kids dived into bathrooms. I made it to the shop door, skidded to a stop, and strolled inside. Wampler was helping one of his ninth-graders sand a coffee table. Two guys, breathing hard, came in behind me. Wampler looked up, surprised. His class had never been so popular.

He was calling roll when the vice principal walked in.

Mr. Ratch eyed all of us carefully. I figured he was looking for someone with a wet shirt, but since he didn't find one, he nodded at Wampler and left.

Until I got to English, I didn't remember about leaving the play tryouts. Ms. Castle remembered. "Another excellent job, J.J.," she said when she dropped my paper on my desk. A-minus. One spelling mistake.

"And," she added, "I'd like to have you stay a few minutes after school."

I stayed in my seat when the bell rang. The kids craned their necks to get a glimpse of me before leaving the room. Ms. Castle perched on the desk in front of me. "Now, tell me. Why didn't you read for the school play?"

"I don't know." I shrugged. "I just didn't feel like being in it."

"Why?"

I didn't want to lie and I didn't want to tell her why. We sat there. She had her legs crossed and they were so close they were distracting me.

"J.J.! Tell me why."

"My old man's in prison for stealing cars."

"That's too bad, but what's that got to do with your walking out on the tryouts?"

"It's got everything to do with it. You think guys like Pete McCartney want to be in a play with me? He knows all about my dad."

Ms. Castle threw out her hands. "Pete McCartney didn't even get a part in the play."

"So? Do you think his friends will want to act with me?"

"They'd be lucky to act with you. You drop into character more easily than any student I've had. You're a chameleon. What a gift."

"Ya, well, maybe I'll use it when I grow up and am in another city." I got out of my seat. "The bus will leave if I don't go now. Thanks for the little talk."

She grabbed my arm. "Wait. Sit down. If you miss your bus, I'll drive you home."

I sat back down, but I wasn't feeling too friendly. It didn't sound as if she had any idea of what it's like to be a prisoner's kid.

"I probably should tell you that I knew about your dad too." She paused a minute to flip her long hair over her shoulder. "Whenever I get a new class, I look through the students' files in the counselor's office."

Great. Just great. "What have they got? His whole history?"

"No. Only a little note from your former principal to the counselor here. So we'd understand if there were times you seemed upset."

I stared out the window. I really wanted to split, but I didn't know how without being rude.

"Pay attention to me, please," she said. "I know your life couldn't have been a picnic, but from an actor's point of view you've got a mother lode."

I turned my head toward her and raised an eyebrow. "A what?"

"A gold mine. Actors believe every tough thing that's happened to them, every experience they've had in life, and everyone they've associated with helps them to understand people's feelings and motivations. The more varied experiences the actors have, the more different characters they can play.

"Now think about it." Ms. Castle leaned forward so I'd be sure to get her point. "Couldn't you play a variety of roles more realistically than most kids? How many peo-

70

ple and events have you been exposed to, and how many has Pete McCartney been exposed to?"

She had me there. Pete was under the thumb of his superstraight mom. I'd been around my dad's friends, Rattler and sleazy Louis. And two years ago I'd been blackmailed by a kid named Troller, who threatened to tell the school about my dad if I didn't pay up. When I'd tried to paste his mouth shut, I'd been collared by his fat father, who was a bigger bully than Troller.

"But," I said to Ms. Castle, "even if having a dad like mine has given me lots of experiences, most people think it's a bad thing."

"That's just one view. You don't have to think of him as a bad man. You can think of him as an adventurous man who has a few flaws." Ms. Castle laughed.

I didn't see anything funny in that.

She hopped down from the desk. "Look, J.J., you can creep around being ashamed of your terrible secret or you can say right out loud, 'Ya, my old man's in prison for rippin' off cars.' Then what have kids got to gossip about?"

I still didn't want to be rude, but I thought there were a few experiences Ms. Castle hadn't had. "You probably had normal parents," I told her.

She laughed again. "Don't you believe it. My parents were alcoholics. Come on. I'll drive you home."

Ms. Castle is the kind of driver that speeds up to make every green light and a few of the yellows. She did stop for the stop signs. She glanced over to me as she shifted gears. "There's another thing I've been wondering about."

"Ya, what?"

"You seem too practiced or experienced when you

71

read a part. Is somebody in your family an actor? Your mother or an aunt?"

This time I laughed. "It's my father. I've been practicing with him for years." Then I broke down and told her about the time a store manager caught Dad just as he was about to go out the door wearing a pair of shoes he hadn't paid for. Dad pretended he was so preoccupied with testing the shoes that he hadn't noticed he'd walked clear over to the store's entrance.

"And what did you do while this was going on?" she asked.

"As soon as I spotted the manager coming, I dropped down to Dad's feet and pretended I was feeling the toes of his shoes to check the fit."

"Ah, a little street drama. Your apprenticeship. You may thank him for your gift someday."

I pointed to the houses ahead of us. "That brown one is mine."

No one can miss Ms. Castle's red convertible. Matt didn't. He was in his driveway tightening the lug nuts on his wheels and almost dropped his wrench when he saw me get out of her car. "Way to go, Johnson," he yelled as I went up my porch steps with a big grin all over my face.

10

Grungy Thief

At four o'clock Grace knocked on my door. I was stretched out on the couch with my hands behind my head. I yelled at her to come in.

She came through the door and took a second take at me. "You sick again?"

"No, I was just thinking about some things Ms. Castle said."

Grace wrinkled her nose at the mention of Ms. Castle. "What did she say now? That you're going to be the next Matt Dillon?"

"Not quite. She said all the scams I watched my dad pull helped me learn how to act. And that I might thank him someday for giving me the gift."

"Thank him!" Grace plopped down into the big chair. "All the trouble he's caused you? He's worse than my mother."

"Oh, I don't know. Ms. Castle may have a point. Maybe living with him left me with some good things."

"Living next door to him left us with a stolen car."

"My dad didn't have anything to do with that. I asked

73

him Sunday and he said everyone he knows is locked up.
It made him feel bad that I thought it was his fault."

"But he was bad!" Grace said.

"I don't have to think of him that way."

She bit on a thumbnail a minute. "He always was
friendly, though. You'd never know he was a robber."

"Ms. Castle says if I didn't make such a big deal out of
his being in prison, it wouldn't be. She says I shouldn't
try to keep it a secret."

"Or maybe you should talk about Willard and his restaurant. He's your dad now."

I wrinkled my nose like Grace does. She giggled.

"So, your mom's up at school."

"Ugh, yes. And I hate to think what she's doing to
me."

I swung my feet to the floor and sat up. "Listen, Grace,
you're doing some of it to yourself. I saw you bawl when
you got wet. And a girl came out right after you and took
a balloon away from Morgan and squirted water all over
those guys."

"What are you talking about!" Grace's blue eyes
flashed like a warning light. "I didn't even see the thing
coming. And that was my new vest."

"Grace! The point is last year you would have given
those guys worse than they gave you. Now you're all
weepy and whiny. What's the matter with you?"

Grace slumped back into the chair. "I don't know. I
don't know. Wearing those dumb clothes made me feel
so dumb. And Summer and all the girls were going
around in shorts."

"But it's too cold to wear shorts now and you've got
jeans like everyone else. I think you've lost your guts.
Part of the time you act like your mom."

"I know. I know." She ripped off a fingernail.

I didn't think I should beat on her anymore, so I said, "Let's go out and toss the basketball around."

We went out in my backyard and played one-on-one. It was a dull game, though. Grace kept worrying about her mom being at the junior high talking to her home-ec teacher, and her shots didn't even come close to the basket.

When we were both winded, I got us a couple of Cokes from the kitchen and we sat outside with our backs against the garage doors. "I think I've figured out what to do," I said.

"What?" Grace asked.

"Tomorrow you go to home ec early and tell Thornsbury you want to talk to her. Then you explain a little about how excited your mom gets and ask Thornsbury if she couldn't please just watch Jenson and Taylor during class time. But not say anything to them about you." I took a swig of Coke and grinned at Grace. "That should do it."

"Maybe." Grace stuck another finger in her mouth and ripped off another fingernail.

"Try it," I urged.

"Well, okay," she said, and finished off her Coke.

I thought I might hear what happened to Grace in PE, but I didn't because we didn't suit up. Ms. Kraft met us at the locker room and told us to go directly into the gym. When we were all there, she announced that we wouldn't be suiting up for the next month because we would be doing square dancing.

Square dancing! Lonewolf and I groaned together.

"Come on, you guys," Ms. Kraft said. "Square dancing can be fun."

Fun! Why would a teacher deliberately ruin the best subject in school? For a whole month? And especially Ms. Kraft. She has thighs like Schwarzenegger.

"Now, let's make three circles of eight students each. Boy, girl, boy, girl. Hold hands. Man's palm up, lady's palm down." Ms. Kraft sang out the last words.

"*Lady's* palm?" I mouthed to Lonewolf. Clarice was hovering near me, so I took one of her hands. I'm five-seven and growing. Clarice is at least five-ten, and I hope she's not still growing.

"Come on, come on." Ms. Kraft moved behind the circles, pulling kids together. "It won't kill you to touch each other."

"That's what she thinks," Lonewolf mouthed back to me as he placed three fingers under Angela's fat paw. Angela tops Lonewolf's weight by at least fifty pounds.

Ms. Kraft moved back to an old record player she had propped up against the gym wall. She put the needle on the record, and the tinny sound of "Yes Sir, That's My Baby" filled the gym. Lonewolf rolled his black eyes away from Angela.

"Everyone watch me." Ms. Kraft rose onto the balls of her feet and, taking little baby steps, shuffled across the floor. Maybe those tiny skips would have looked okay if she'd been wearing a long skirt instead of gym shorts. And if the whistle hanging down her gray sweatshirt hadn't bounced from one big bulge to the other with every skip she took.

Kathy was holding Lonewolf's left hand. She giggles all the time anyway and was bent double by the time Ms. Kraft had shuffled back to the wall. Lonewolf yanked

Kathy up straight while Ms. Kraft carefully took the needle off the record.

"Everyone bend elbows so your circles are round." Ms. Kraft evened out the spaces between the kids that had one arm stretched out farther than the other. "Now, turn the bottom half of your body to the right. Take short steps, moving from your knees down. Go!"

I banged into Clarice, who was skipping to the left.

"Stop," Ms. Kraft yelled. "Right, right. You're moving to the right. Go!

"Good! Now turn to the left. Left! Left!"

It took fifteen minutes before we all went to the right or left at Ms. Kraft's command. But when she put on the record and sang out stuff like, "Turn the other way back. Circle to the left now going around the track," half the kids crashed into the other half.

Five minutes before the class was over, she tried to teach us how to bow and curtsy. "Men, your partner is the lady on your right. To acknowledge your partner, you hold your lady's left hand with your right one and put your right foot by her left foot. Take a step back on your left foot. Bend your left knee, pointing your right foot, and bow from the waist.

"Ladies, hold your bodies straight and curtsy by bending both your knees. Let's go. This should be easy enough for you all to do."

Sure.

The bell ended total confusion. What a wasted gym period. But it made my English class a blast.

After we'd finished our spelling test, Ms. Castle played a tape of Rich Little's imitations. She told us she'd give us ten minutes to come up with an imitation of our own. "Choose a president or actor the way Rich Little did. Or choose one of the school staff," she said. "We want to be able to guess who you're imitating. Try to remember how the principal walks and talks. Or the cook. Or me."

Or Ms. Kraft! I rolled up my pant legs, balled up two wads of paper and stuffed them under my T-shirt, and waited for my turn. Most of the kids ahead of me did miserable copies of Rich Little. Clarice didn't. She imitated the janitor making a girl erase four-letter words off her ex-boyfriend's locker door. I was surprised that she could be so funny.

When my turn came, I sang out, "Now circle round the track," and, taking little tiny skips, I shuffled from the windows to the blackboard to the wall. Every kid who'd had gym that day was falling in the aisles, but Ms. Castle didn't get it. Clarice explained it to her.

Ms. Castle ended the class by suggesting that those who were good at this sort of thing might try practicing in front of a mirror. And, she said, we could check out the callboards on the theater page in the local newspapers to see if there were open calls for juvenile actors.

I was still all hopped up about that idea when Grace and I got off the bus. "I'm going to look in the Sunday paper for open calls," I told her. "That means anybody can read for a part."

"You think a theater is going to hire some kid?" she snapped.

"Of course. People have kids. So people in plays have kids."

"Fascinating."

I took a sidelong glance at her drooping mouth. "What happened in home ec?"

"Just like your English class. It was a blast."

"Did you see Thornsbury before class?"

78

"Yes, that was a great idea. She didn't even look up from her grade book when she told me that I needn't be concerned about the boys any longer and to please take my seat."

"Whoa, your mother must have really given it to her."

"Probably."

I kicked at some of the wet maple leaves that were stuck to the sidewalk. I didn't really want to ask Grace any more questions. I knew I was going to hear bad news if I did, but I felt sorry for her. "So, what did Jenson and Taylor act like when they came in?"

"They were laughing and knocking each other around. The usual."

That's where I should have dropped it. I didn't, though. I said, "Well, what happened?"

"Oh, Ms. Thornsbury called roll and then the vice principal came on the PA and said he wanted to see Michael Jenson and Phillip Taylor in his office."

I took another quick glance at Grace. We were almost home and for sure she was going to cry. Her chin was tilted up, but her droopy mouth was quivering.

"They got in trouble, huh?" I said.

"I wouldn't know. They didn't tell me what happened when they came back to class. They don't come near me. And neither does anybody else."

"Oh, come on. It isn't that bad."

Grace whirled around. We were in front of her house and by now her face was wet with tears, but she planted her feet on her walkway, clutched her book bag to her chest, and gave it to me anyway. "What do you know? You weren't there. And if it wasn't for you, I wouldn't be in this mess. You had to go sneaking off to my dad and

79

complain about my clothes and make my mother mad enough to go to school. You should have butted out."

I backed up to the grass on the parking strip. "Hey, wait a minute. You were the one sniveling about the clothes your mother made you wear."

"My mother just wanted me to look like a lady, and if you'd kept your mouth shut, I would have gotten her to buy me some jeans."

"Jeez, why didn't you, then? And how many times have you talked to your father about me?"

"If I hadn't, you would have stayed a grungy little thief like your dad." By the way she jerked her head back, I knew she knew what she'd done. That didn't cut any ice.

I stared at her for a couple seconds before I said, "Drop dead, Grace."

11

Sorry

I paced around my living room chomping on the turkey sandwich Mom had left in the refrigerator for me. Between bites I muttered curses on Grace. If there were any guys living in the neighborhood, I wouldn't have had to listen to her blubber about her dorky clothes. So much for feeling sorry for someone.

I kept pacing even when I'd finished my sandwich. *Jeez,* what a stupid girl. She dumped all her problems on me and then called me a grungy thief. With her loony mother, she had a lot of guts talking about my dad.

The sandwich left me feeling sticky, but when I tried to wipe my face, my hand slid across my mouth. Mayonnaise. I split for the bathroom to wash it off.

After I put the towel back on the hook, I checked my face in the mirror. Hmmm. I could make one side of my mouth droop like Grace's did before she cried, but it took practice to get both corners drooping. And then getting the quiver down. That took a while.

"Hey, Clarice," I said when I got to the gym the next day. "Watch me. What am I going to do?"

"Cry," she said.

"Right!" I said.

"Now watch me." Clarice swayed like she was drunk. Her eyes narrowed until they focused on me. Her lower jaw slowly slid forward, her guts hardened, and her fist clenched.

"You're going to slug me," I guessed.

Clarice shook her head. "Naw, I'm going to knock my kid across the room."

Whoa. While we practiced our bows and curtsies, I wondered what kind of scary life she had.

Ms. Castle must have wondered the same thing. As soon as we got in her class, Clarice asked her to watch me. I did Grace's mouth quiver and Ms. Castle laughed. "You look like a girl getting ready to cry."

"He's trying to," Clarice said. "Now watch this."

Ms. Castle's eyes widened as Clarice went into her mean-drunk routine. "Who've you been associating with?" she asked when Clarice was finished. "You're so real you're scary."

That's what I'd thought. Clarice just smiled, though, like it was a good joke on us.

By now half the class was crowded around Ms. Castle's desk. "Everybody'd better take their seats," she said. "We've got a reading-comprehension test today."

Reading comprehension, ugh.

On the way out of Ms. Castle's room I checked the play list that was posted beside her door. Pete's name wasn't on it, but Clarice's was. I didn't even remember seeing her at the tryouts.

I thought about Clarice's imitations while I rode home

82

on the bus. She managed to use her whole body instead of just her face. I imagined walking bowlegged like Rattler. He's a little skinny man, but he holds his arms out wide as if his bulging muscles keep them from touching his sides. He probably got his name from his gravelly voice, but he should be called Popeye.

Grace got off the bus before I did. She stopped to pull her hood over her head because it was raining again. I waited on the curb until she was a third of the way down the block. Even then I was bound to catch up with her. She was creeping along so slowly.

When I was about three feet away, I speeded up and went right by her. She wasn't getting a chance to say one word to me. I went directly into my house, grabbed a Coke, and walked around the kitchen bowlegged with my arms held out from my sides.

Sunday morning I bushied up my eyebrows with Mom's brown pencil and twisted my face around in the mirror until I got a scowl like Rattler's. I was just getting Rattler's voice down when Mom opened the bathroom door. "Jerry! What in the world is going on?"

"I'm just practicing imitations," I explained.

Mom had one hand over her heart. "Good Lord, you scared me to death. I thought . . ."

"You thought Rattler was in here?" I asked hopefully.

"It isn't funny," she said. "Get out of here so I can go to the bathroom."

She was still in her nightgown. I read the Sunday paper until she was dressed and had breakfast ready. Willard gulped his coffee and frowned at me because I'd kept the middle of the paper. "How come you're not reading the funnies?" he asked.

83

"I already did," I told him. "I'm checking the entertainment section to see if there's a call for juveniles."

"Actors?" he said. "You want to be an actor? I hope you know the probability of that idea being profitable is near zero."

I lowered my eyelids to half-mast. "Everyone's welcome to an opinion."

Mrs. Beasley was late for class on Monday. The other history teacher stuck her head in our door and said Mrs. Beasley was taking a long-distance call and would be along in a minute. In the meantime we were to read our books quietly. My big chance.

I minced up the aisle with my hips stuck out in back and my chest pouched out in front. I picked up a manila file from Beasley's desk, turned around, and peered at the kids from over the top of the file. "Stu-dents," I said in Beasley's high, wavering voice, "I've been checking over your school records. Clayton, I see that both your parents are Boeing engineers. I certainly hope that doesn't mean your mother's one of those feminists who smokes brown cigarettes."

"No, ma'am," Clayton said. "She smokes five-dollar cigars."

"And Summer Day, dear, I see you have a younger sister and brother. I certainly hope their names aren't Spring and Winter."

Summer tried to get an answer in a couple times, but she was laughing too hard.

I smeared a sickly-sweet smile across my face. "And Lonewolf, you poor little redskin. I've noticed that your watchband is made of turquoise stones. I really don't

84

think it looks masculine for boys to wear jewelry to school."

That got a big grin out of Lonewolf.

I turned to Lindsi. "Dear, will you please run down the hall and tell the AV boy that we need a film projector. Stu-dents, I'm going to give you a special treat. While I rest my tiny buffalo butt in one of your seats, you all are going to watch *Bear Country* for the twenty-fourth time in your school career. I hope—"

Clayton loudly cleared his throat. Everyone's eyes shifted to the door. I turned to smile at Mrs. Beasley. "We were just having a class discussion."

"Yes, well, I heard the laughter when I was halfway up the hall. I really think all of you should be mature enough to read your books quietly for five minutes. And, Jerry, you've clowned around enough for today. Please take your seat."

I put the manila folder back on her desk and took my seat, amazed that she didn't chew me out for having the file. She told us to read the chapter on the history of the city of Snohomish. While we read, she sat at her desk and stared out the window.

As soon as Beasley dismissed us, Grace called up the aisle, "Gol, you were funny, Jerry."

I ignored her.

Summer walked with me to the door. "I wonder if Mrs. Beasley's phone call was bad news. She seems so un-happy. Maybe someone in her family is sick."

I took a glance back at Beasley. She did look pretty miserable, all right, but it was strange thinking of Old B.B. having a family.

The next Sunday I checked the *Times* again. There wasn't even a callboard in it. The next Monday Grace gave up dragging her feet so I could catch up with her. She turned to face me. "Jerry, I'm sorry I—"

"Forget it, Grace," I said, and shrugged her off.

After school Wednesday I emptied our mailbox. There was a flyer from Safeway, a phone bill, a letter from Dad, and a letter from Grace. Grace??

I read Dad's letter first. He said he'd made such a good record in the reformatory so far that he thought he might get on work release for the last part of his sentence. I didn't know about that. He always did fine when someone was standing over him, but as soon as he was on his own, he goofed up. He intended to be good and he would be until something came along that he wanted to do and then he just did it. Without thinking about the consequences.

The last part of his letter was about my visit. About how the guys who saw me thought I looked just like him. "You're everything a man could want in a son," he wrote. "Please don't forget me, my boy. Love, yr dad."

Why did he keep worrying that I'd forget him? It made him sound so lonely. But then I guessed I was all he had.

I dropped his letter down the corner of the seat cushion and tore open Grace's envelope. A newspaper clipping fell out and onto the rug. I left it there.

Grace has round, loopy handwriting that goes clear across the page. My dad's sentences kind of waver up and down. She started out her letter apologizing for blaming her troubles on me.

Dear Jerry,

I'm sorry I blamed you for my troubles. I *am really really* sorry. I was upset because Mike and

86

Phil walk all the way around the back of the room so they never have to pass my desk. And the other kids watch them and do what they do. Ms. Thornsbury doesn't come by me unless she has to. Anyway I know you don't want to hear any more about my troubles.

She was right about that. I didn't even want to finish reading her letter. But I did.

My uncle came to see us over the weekend, and he left a copy of the *Seattle Weekly* in the bedroom. This ad was in it. I thought you might be interested.

I didn't mean to say anything about your dad. Especially since you helped save Matt's car from a real thief.

I'm really sorry. Sorry. Sorry. Sorry!

Grace

I picked up the ad from the floor.

Callboard

Commercial—Open call for male juvenile performers age 12 to 14. Call 555-3366 for appointment.

Whoa! I leapt across the room, grabbed the phone, and dialed the number.

"Northwest Productions," a lady said.

I stumbled around trying to tell her I'd read her ad and wanted a tryout.

"How old are you?" she asked.

"Thirteen."

"Have one of your parents call me tomorrow morning for an appointment."

"Okay," I said. "What's your name?"

"Just have them ask for Judith. I'll be here."

"Right. Thanks." I hung up and whirled back across the room and into the kitchen to paste Mom a note on the refrigerator. It said to be sure, sure, sure she called Northwest Productions as soon as she got up in the morning.

12

One Smokin' Buggy

The bus was late. I teetered on the curb looking down the road for it. Grace huddled in her slicker behind me. It'd stopped raining, but she had her hood pulled over her head anyway.

She seemed shrunken, like the power had seeped out of her. I had a feeling that when I'd told her to drop dead, the last of the old Grace crumbled. The "grungy little thief" crack still burned, but my resolve to make her eat it was melting. "Wonder where the bus is," I said.

"Maybe it had a flat," Grace mumbled.

"Maybe."

Silence behind me. I hated feeling sorry for her. She deserved what she got. Like her dad'd told me once, people were responsible for their decisions. And she'd ratted on Jenson and Taylor and called me a thief.

I didn't know whether to go back home or stay on the curb waiting for the bus. If I went home, I could be there when Mom called Northwest Productions. But if Judith did give me an appointment, it'd be because of Grace.

89

I turned around. "Well, what do you think? Shall we bag it?"

"I don't know." She took a quick peek at my face. Her blue eyes were rimmed with red.

I checked my watch. "Well, maybe we should wait another five minutes."

Grace's hood nodded. She'd pulled inside it again like a turtle.

I decided I might as well tell her I'd left a note for Mom to call about the commercial. I wanted her to be sorry for blaming me for her troubles, but I didn't want her stomped into the ground. I'd just opened my mouth to speak, when the bus came in sight.

"Hurry up. Hurry up. We're late," the bus driver called out the door.

"No kidding," I said as I climbed up the steps. "What happened anyway?"

"The Snohomish River's overflowing. We had to take a detour." He almost slammed the door on the back of Grace's slicker before he took off down the road.

After school I waited for Grace to hop down the bus steps. "Let's go check out the river," I said.

"I can't. My mom screamed at Matt last night because he and some other guys raced their cars through the water on Highway 9. She said we were both to stay away from the flood."

"It won't be dangerous now. The river's probably crested."

"I know." It was just sprinkling out, but Grace was still hiding under her hood.

"How'd your mom find out about Matt?"

"The usual. Gossiping on the phone."

"How'd he get new wheels?"

"My grandma."

Bringing her out from under her hood was going to take more than talking about her brother. "How about coming over to my house," I suggested. "My mom's probably called on that ad you gave me and we can find out if I got an appointment for a tryout."

She stopped at her walkway. "I can't. Mom's home." Grace is never allowed to come in my house unless my folks are there. She does if her mom isn't home, though.

"Well, I'll see ya," I told her.

"Um, Jerry." Grace stared straight at me for the first time that day. "If you do get a tryout, I'll go with you. If you want me to."

"Sure. I could use some company. I'll be nervous."

I was nervous at the tryout, all right. But Grace didn't keep me company. Mom did. My appointment was for ten o'clock Friday morning and Grace's mother wouldn't let her skip school.

The production office looked about the same as a dentist's waiting room. Magazines were on low tables beside rows of chairs. Judith's desk was next to a door. The door led to the tryout room, I guessed.

Mom filled out a bunch of papers Judith gave her while I squirmed on one of the chairs. I'd already gone to the bathroom once and I wondered if I should go again before they called my name. Two kids had been called in ahead of me, but only one had come back. When the kid's mom looked up at him, he shook his head, so I figured he didn't make it.

"Here, Jerry," Judith said. "You might want to read this over while you're waiting. We give it to all our young actors. We don't want their faces breaking out before a shoot."

I got up and took the paper she held out. Her fingernails were long and red, and dangly green earrings flashed below her short hair. Great big gray eyes with curly lashes made her so pretty I couldn't return her smile.

I sat back down thinking *she* should be on TV, then looked at the paper in my hand.

> FOR A GOOD APPEARANCE, AVOID THESE
>   FOODS:
>   Avoid fried foods. Choose chicken or fish that
>   is baked, broiled, or stewed.
>   Avoid sweets, especially chocolate.
>   Avoid pop. Drink fruit juice instead.
>   Avoid snacks like potato and corn chips. Eat fruit,
>   vegetable sticks, or raw nuts.

Mom had given her papers back to Judith, so I handed her the list. "What are those?" I whispered, pointing to the vegetable sticks.

"Little pieces of carrots or celery," she whispered back.

I frowned at Mom. Eat pieces of carrots instead of chips? And what about fries? They're the best thing at McDonald's. I could just see myself going up to the counter and asking for a fishburger with raw nuts.

A buzzer sounded on Judith's desk. "You can go in now, Jerry," she told me.

What about the boy who hadn't come out?

I saw him as soon as I opened the door. He was sitting in a chair tipped back against the side wall. A man and a woman sat at a small table littered with papers. Another man with his hair in a ponytail was behind the camera.

"You're Gerald Johnson, Junior." The man at the table was reading my name off one of the papers in front of him.

"Yes, sir," I said.

"Stand behind that white mark on the floor. When the camera rolls, say your name. And then I want you to pretend you see a beautiful car coming down the street. React to the sight of the car and say anything that seems natural to you. Questions?"

"No," I said.

"All right, let's go."

I walked to the middle of the room, stood behind the mark, and looked toward the camera. When I saw the cameraman push a button, I said, "Jerry Johnson, Junior." I almost corrected myself by saying, I mean *Gerald* Johnson, Junior, but I remembered Ms. Castle told us to keep going even if we made a mistake.

I imagined Matt's car passing by, turned my head a little, widened my eyes, and gave out a low whistle. "Whoa! One smokin' buggy!"

No one said anything after the cameraman took his finger off the button. The woman stared at me thoughtfully. Did I do good or did I do lousy? I was about to move off the mark when the man at the table nodded to the boy lounging in the chair. "Do a take with him."

The boy joined me in front of the camera. The man told us to say our names and to imagine a beautiful car going by again.

The boy said, "Nigel Tobin."

I said, "Gerald Johnson, Junior."

Then I swiveled my head as if I were watching a car. "Check out that cool black Camaro."

Nigel said, "Firebirds are sweet cars."

"Naw, Firebirds are a bunch of junk," I said. "That Camaro's smokin'."

The cameraman let go of the button. He was laughing silently. I didn't get it.

The man at the table got up and clapped me on the shoulder. "Camaros and Firebirds are the same cars, son. We'll look at your tapes and make a decision. Thanks for coming in."

I went out the door feeling like a fool. Nigel stayed in there. While Mom put on her coat, Judith told the next kid to go in.

"Well, how'd you do?" Mom asked when we were in the hall.

"Terrible." I pushed the down button for the elevator.

"What went wrong, honey?"

The elevator doors opened. It was crowded with people. We crammed in the front.

"What went wrong?" Mom asked again as we walked along Union Street in downtown Seattle.

"Wait until we get in the car."

She gave me a questioning look as she drove her car out of the parking garage. I made her wait until she was through the traffic and going down I-5. "I thought a Camaro was different than a Firebird," I said.

"What? What has that got to do with your test for the commercial?"

"Tryout, Mom."

"Well, I don't understand."

So I told her. Everything that happened. And how the cameraman had laughed.

94

"Jerry, the names of the cars don't make any difference. It's how you acted. It sounds like you did all right to me. In fact it sounds as if you were more animated than that Nigel."

"Maybe," I said, "but I think he's already chosen."

"They must be planning on two of you."

"Maybe," I said again, and took my thumb out of my mouth. I'd been ripping at my nails the way Grace does.

13

Action!

Saturday morning Willard saw the list on the coffee table. "What's this?" he said. "Those TV people think they know how to cook?"

I didn't answer him. Neither did Mom. Willard's specialty is fried oysters.

After they left for the restaurant, I sat down and wrote a long letter to Dad. I told him all about the tryout and how I'd made a fool of myself when Nigel said Firebirds are sweet cars and I said Firebirds were a bunch of junk compared with Camaros. I felt better after I'd finished the letter. Making the cameraman laugh no longer seemed like such a big deal.

Willard didn't need me at work until six o'clock that night. I thought of going over to Grace's until then. But I decided to do homework instead.

Monday morning she asked a million questions about what had happened at the production company. She was blabbering like the old Grace except she kept saying, "Oh, I just know they'll call you." It seemed as if the power had shifted from her to me and she was knocking herself out to please me.

I didn't talk to anyone else about my tryout. I thought about telling Clarice, but Ms. Kraft kept us busy learning allemande left and do-si-do. She called for a ladies' choice near the end of class. Luckily Clarice chose me. Kathy and her friends knew about my dad. It'd fix them if I got on TV.

I hurried home after school, sat in the big chair, and stared at the phone. "Ring," I said to it, "Ring." Three days later it rang.

"Hello, Jerry, this is Judith."

"Hi," I croaked. My pounding heart was choking me.

"We have a job for you. It's on the twenty-eighth of this month. Can you make it?"

"Sure."

"We'll want you to be at Forty-third and Tenth Avenue in the University District at seven o'clock. Can you get up that early?"

"No sweat."

"Bring along several outfits. Jeans, running shoes, sweaters, shirts to wear under your sweater. Nothing that's black or white."

"Not even my shoes?"

"It'll be all right if your shoes are black or white. Not your clothes, though. Karen will be there to help you and Nigel with your wardrobes. I guess that's all. Oh, your mother will have to be there to sign a contract with the ad agency."

"She will be," I said.

"Fine. Have her give me a call tomorrow. Good luck on your shoot."

98

I hung up the phone and took a big breath after a big breath. Whoa! Whoa! I couldn't believe it was happening to me. The convict's kid was going on TV. Wow!

I whipped around the room going, "Wow! Wow!" My grade-school principal had said she'd see me on TV someday. But it was a daydream. A maybe-someday daydream. This was real. Real. Wow!

I had to tell someone. I wanted to tell Mom, but Willard answered the phone. "You can't talk to your mother now, Jerry. She's waiting tables."

"You jerk!" I wanted to say. "She could come to the phone for a second." Instead I told him to tell Mom I had the job for the commercial. I hung up right after I said this. That'd show the old coot with his zero probability of my making money as an actor.

How much money? I wondered. How much money do they pay you? Maybe a hundred dollars?

I grabbed my jacket and went over to Grace's house. Her mother answered the door, obviously not delighted to see me. But when Grace started screaming, "You got it! You got it! I knew you would," Mrs. Elliott hurried back into the living room.

"What have you got, Jerry?"

"A part in a TV commercial."

"Oh."

I could almost see the wheels spinning in Mrs. Elliott's head. Wasn't I going to turn out like my father after all? "What are you going to be advertising?" she asked cautiously.

"I don't know for sure. I tried out for a car advertisement. That might be what it is."

"My, that would be nice."

99

"Nice!" Grace screamed. "It's fabulous. Jerry's going to be famous. And *I* gave him the notice about the job!"

I thanked Grace for giving me the callboard ad. And when Mom got home from work, I thanked her for taking me to the tryout. Her eyes were glowing. "I'll take you to every one of them, honey."

Willard gave me a small smile and nod. I think he was waiting to see how big my check was before he went overboard.

Clarice didn't scream as loud as Grace and her eyes didn't glow as bright as Mom's, but she was sure interested. "Now, wait a minute," she said after I answered "Here!" to Ms. Kraft's roll call. "Wait a minute. Exactly where was this notice? I didn't see anything like that in the *Everett Herald* or the *Seattle Times*."

"It was in the *Seattle Weekly*," I said. "A friend found it for me."

"I'll ask my dad to bring home the *Weekly*. I didn't even think of that."

"Get in a circle, you two," Ms. Kraft ordered. "We've got dancin' to do."

When I got to English class, Clarice was already telling Ms. Castle about my job. "Congratulations, J.J." Ms. Castle took my hand and held it a minute. "Your dad will be so proud."

I hadn't really thought of that. My dad hadn't had much to be proud of in his life.

There was a letter from him in the mailbox when I got home. "Not everybody knows that Firebirds and Camaros have the same chassis, so don't sweat that," he had written. "But I think you'd better watch that kid, Nigel. He might have been trying to throw you." Dad went on to tell me that he was sure I could beat out the competition easy. And that he loved me.

Every once in a while in the next two weeks I worried about Dad's warning. It was strange that Nigel had just popped out with the word *Firebird.* I worried about what to wear too.

Mom stayed home the night before the shoot and went through my closet with me. We chose a red crew and a yellow turtleneck sweater, a light-blue T-shirt, a green-plaid shirt, and dark-blue jeans. I sure hoped they were the right choices.

Mom took forever getting ready in the morning. Willard was up and fixing breakfast. That was a first. When Mom came in the kitchen, Willard smiled. "You going on TV too?"

"Well, I don't want Jerry to be ashamed of me."

"Ashamed of you?" I stared at her over my glass of orange juice. "You're prettier than any other mother. Take Grace's, for instance."

"I'd rather not," she said.

Willard gave her an extra pat on the cheek after she kissed him good-bye. I guess they had something going, but it was hard to imagine bald old Willard as a match for my mom.

There was a van and a truck with a boom on it parked on the barricaded street when we got to the University District. Nigel and his dad drove up behind us. Mom and Mr. Tobin introduced themselves while Nigel and I checked out the yellow Chrysler convertible that was in the middle of the road.

I put out my hand to feel the tan leather seats.

"Hey, kid! Don't touch that car!" the driver yelled from the curb.

101

"Neat buggy," I mumbled to Nigel.

"It should be," Nigel said. "Maserati built it."

I didn't say anything more. Just backed up and took in the fancy wheels.

A lady wearing a bandanna over her hair joined us. "Hi, Nigel. Jerry, I'm Karen. I'll be helping you with your wardrobe and makeup."

Makeup?

"Why don't we go in the van," Karen said, "and get you two dressed."

Karen looked over Nigel's clothes first. She chose blue sweats for him and then the red crew for me. I was relieved when she went out of the van to let us change alone.

"You do many commercials?" I asked Nigel.

"Usually six or seven a year." He'd pulled on his sweats and was combing his hair in the mirror, which hung above the side seats.

"How much do they pay you?"

"A little over two hundred." Nigel poked his head forward and examined his teeth in the mirror. I wished he'd get out of the way so I could see if I looked all right.

Karen came back in, opened her makeup kit, and made Nigel sit down while she drew on his blond eyebrows with a light brown pencil. "I think we'll bring out your freckles more this time."

Nigel started to say something, but she clapped his mouth closed by bumping his chin with her knuckles. "Hold still."

I was careful to hold still while she did me. I was afraid she'd put lipstick on us. She didn't. But she did powder our faces. "To keep the shine down," she explained.

When she was finished, she called in the director to

102

check us over. He said we looked fine and handed each of us a paper. "Memorize these lines," he told us. "We should be ready for you in about an hour."

"An hour?" I said to Nigel after he and Karen had left. "What are they going to do for an hour?"

"Set the camera up, measure distances, mark the street, check the sun. All that stuff. You'll get used to waiting. Mostly all we do is wait."

He was right. Even when they had us out on the sidewalk going through our lines, we were stopped every few minutes for the camera to make an adjustment, for the mike to be raised, for the car to be polished. Once I pulled my sweater out from my chest to cool off while the convertible was being wheeled back to its starting point.

I'd barely gotten my sweater out an inch when Karen rushed up to me. "Never, never touch your clothes, Jerry. You have to appear absolutely the same in every take." She adjusted my sweater, smoothed my hair, and went back to the sidelines, keeping a beady eye on me. Nigel smirked. I didn't like him much.

After everything was finally ready, the director gave us our instructions. "When I say 'Action,' you begin. Don't stop until I say 'Cut.' Don't even stop if you make a mistake. Keep going until you hear 'Cut.' "

He backs up, yells "Action," the convertible rolls up the street, Nigel and I walk down the sidewalk. "Cancel all my Christmases," Nigel says. "But just let me have that beauty for a week."

I turn my head to see what Nigel is talking about. A big grin spreads over my face when I spot the beautiful car. "Wow! That is one me-ean machine!" The yellow convertible rolls by us. We stare after it with worshipful expressions.

103

"Cut," the director yells. He confers with the camera-man. The driver backs up the convertible to its starting mark. We wait. And wait. And wait.

"Okay," the director says. "Again. Action!"

The car rolls, we walk, Nigel cancels Christmas, I say that's one me-ean machine. The director yells, "Cut!"

We do this over and over. Except for Nigel stumbling into me once, as far as I can tell we never mess up. But the cameraman doesn't like the cloud going over the sun and casting a shadow on the car and the director doesn't like it when the woman across the street comes down her front steps or when an airplane flies overhead and the boom mike picks up the sound.

About the ninth time I'm sure it can't be more perfect. But the director doesn't yell, "Okay, folks, that's it," until we've done twelve takes. He thanks me and Nigel.

Nigel and I go into the van to wipe our faces. When I come out, Mom is signing a paper for a lady in a gray suit. As we walk to our car, I whisper to Mom, "How much did I make?"

Mom squeezes my arm and whispers back, "Within thirty days you'll receive a check for two hundred twenty-one dollars and seventy-six cents."

"Yowee!" I yell, and yank our car door open. "Let's go get hamburgers and fries. I'm starved."

But as she maneuvers the car around the barricade at the end of the street, I have second thoughts and ask Mom, "Is there a restaurant around here where I can order broiled chicken and pineapple juice?"

14

She's Not Perfect

I knew Willard would be impressed with the money I earned for the commercial. And he was. Grace was too. "Gol," she said on the way to school the next morning, "what are you going to spend it on?"

"I'm going to save it for a car. But if I get any more jobs, Mom wants me to put part of my pay in a housing fund she and Willard have."

"That's a good idea. I bet she's sick of renting that old place. And I bet you can't wait until Summer sees you on TV. Are you going to tell her and Clayton in history today?"

Actually I was hoping she'd tell them. Then I could just sit back and watch.

Instead she said, "I wish I were going to be there to see their faces."

"How come you're not?" I wanted to know.

"Mom's picking me up at ten o'clock to take me to the dentist. Anyway I won't have to go to home ec."

"Jenson and Taylor aren't still bothering you."

"No. No. They don't bother me. They don't speak to

me." The way she lifted her chin made me suddenly feel bad. But there was nothing more I could do for her. She'd just have to stick it out.

I got into the history class before Beasley did. Summer was already in her seat. Before I slid into mine, I said, "I'm going to be on TV a week from Sunday."

Summer turned around, her green eyes opened wide. "You are? How come?"

"I'm going to be in a car commercial."

"You're going to *what*?" Clayton had halted in the middle of the aisle and so had Russell.

"I tried out for a part in a TV commercial and got it," I told them. "And yesterday we filmed it."

"You're kidding," Russell said.

"Aw right!" Clayton high-fived me. "What make?"

"Chrysler. The car we used was a yellow convertible TC. Built by Maserati."

"You're kidding," Russell said again.

Beasley bustled into the room. "Stu-dents! Let's get settled quickly. We have lots of material to review today. I'm sure you all want to pass your test tomorrow on Snohomish County."

She could be sure Clayton did. He sat down immediately. With his straight A's Clayton planned to be at the top of the junior high honor roll.

I half listened as Beasley went over the history of the Snohomish River from the steamboats to the first Avenue D bridge and then over the fight about the site of the county courthouse. When Beasley said the courthouse was built in Everett in 1890, Clayton's hand shot up.

"Yes, Clayton."

"I thought the courthouse was started in the city of Snohomish in 1890 and finished in 1891."

106

"No, it was built in Everett in 1890."

Clayton looked doubtful and Beasley looked annoyed. I wrote down *Snohomish County Courthouse—Everett—1890.* I guess Clayton and the rest of the class did too.

Beasley went on to Snohomish's Chinese problem, and I spaced out until the bell rang. I was awake, though, when I hit the gym. I grabbed skinny Clarice around her waist. "We shot the commercial yesterday and I'm on TV a week from Sunday."

She gave me a hug right there in front of Kraft and Kathy and the rest of the kids. "Jerry! I'll watch it. I'll tape it! You lucky—" She stopped herself, remembering where she was.

I laughed. Clarice obviously doesn't come from any preacher's family and neither does her vocabulary.

Ms. Kraft called roll. Kathy was looking at me thoughtfully while her name was called. "Kathy?" Ms. Kraft repeated.

"Oh, ya, here," Kathy said.

When I got into English, Clarice and ten other kids were crowded around Ms. Castle's desk. All of them bug-eyed. "So, J.J., you've been filmed," Ms. Castle said.

"We did it yesterday," I said.

"Everyone will want to hear about your adventure. After I pass out the results of the reading tests, we'll have you come up in front and give us a minute-by-minute account."

"Okay, but a minute-by-minute account will be boring. Mostly you stand around and wait."

"Won't bore me," Clarice said.

I got C's on my reading tests and crumpled up the papers. This shot my hope for ever getting an A in English.

"All right, J.J. Let's hear your story." Ms. Castle beamed as I walked to the front of the room. I guess she didn't care if I wasn't an honor student.

I started at the beginning. The truck and van, the barricaded street. The director and his instructions not to stop for anything until he said "Cut."

"That's just what Ms. Castle told us," Clarice put in.

"I know," I said. "And you have to stand on your mark like in play tryouts."

I went on to tell them about Karen and Nigel and the yellow convertible, and when I was finished, Clarice said, "Nigel sounds like a conceited jerk."

"Well," Ms. Castle said, "what actors have to sell is themselves. Chrysler wouldn't film a car that was dirty or dented. Actors can get preoccupied with keeping themselves in shape for the camera."

"Some actors," Clarice replied. "Other actors don't care how bad they look just so they get their characters across."

"True," Ms. Castle agreed, "and those are called character actors."

That's what Clarice and I would be, I thought.

The news that I was going on TV spread around the school fast. By the next morning kids who weren't even in my classes said hi. Mrs. Beasley took an extra-sharp look at me when she passed out our tests on Snohomish County. I figured she knew, but I didn't know what she thought.

I didn't know much on the test, either, but I did remember the answer to number five.

5. In what city was the first Snohomish County Courthouse built in 1890?
   A. Edmonds
   B. Snohomish
   C. Everett
   D. Marysville

Easy. I circled letter C.

"How'd you do on the test?" Grace asked on the way home.

"Lousy. The only thing I know I got right was that the Everett courthouse was built in 1890."

Grace stared up at me. "No, it wasn't. That's when the Snohomish courthouse was built."

"You're wrong, PK. Clayton asked Beasley about it and she said that the Everett courthouse was built in 1890, and I wrote it down."

Grace stopped in the middle of the sidewalk, took her history book out of her bag, and opened it to page 104. "There! See the picture. And right under it it says, 'The Snohomish County Courthouse, City of Snohomish, 1890.' "

I grabbed the book away from her and read the description for myself. She was right. I gave her back her book. "Old Buffalo Butt must have been confused."

"Or you were."

"No, I wasn't and she better not mark my answer wrong."

"She'll have to," Grace said.

Beasley puts the grades on papers in big red letters. I watched as she passed them out. Russell turned his

109

paper over fast so I figured he'd flunked. Clayton stared at his paper in disbelief. A big red B. That'd knock him off the top of the honor roll.

Beasley gave Grace one of her sickeningly sweet smiles. "Very good, Grace."

Grace held her paper up for me to see. A big red A. I got a big red D-minus and turned my paper over. Summer got a C.

"Any questions?" Beasley asked when she was back in front of the room.

Half the class held up their hands.

Beasley called on Robbie.

Robbie stood up. "You told us on Wednesday that the Snohomish County Courthouse was built in Everett in 1890 and that's what I put on my paper, and you marked it wrong."

"It is wrong," Beasley said. "The first courthouse was built in the city of Snohomish in 1890."

"But you told us on Wednesday—"

"No. Just sit down and look in your book. There's a picture of the courthouse in the city of Snohomish and the caption states clearly that it was built in 1890."

Robbie wilted into her seat.

"Any more questions?"

Most of the kids took their hands down, but Clayton kept his raised.

"Clayton?"

"I took notes on your review Wednesday and I have here that you said the courthouse was built in Everett in 1890."

Beasley shook her head. "I can't speak for the way you take notes, Clayton, but if you will also look in your book, you'll see that the correct answer is the city of Snohomish."

"I know. That's what I read too. And that's why I asked you about it Wednesday. And when you said Everett's was built in 1890, that's what I wrote down and that's the answer I thought you'd expect on the test."

Beasley didn't take that well. Her face swelled up and her eyes got little. "I expect you to put the correct answer on your test, young man. And the correct answer is Snohomish."

Clayton shut up. What else could he say? What else could anybody say? The room sat in clammy silence while Beasley turned her back on us to write our next assignment on the blackboard.

"Mrs. Beasley," Grace called out.

Beasley turned around. "Yes?"

"I was absent on Wednesday so I didn't hear the review and I just studied from my book. If I got the answer right and everybody else got it wrong, then maybe you did make a mistake and tell the class it was Everett."

Beasley stared at Grace. I know Grace and I could tell she was scared, but she hung in there and stared right back at her. "Well," Beasley said. "Well, how many of you circled Everett for number five?"

All our hands went up.

"I don't really see how I could have told you Everett, but of course I'm not perfect. Pass your papers up to the front and I'll throw question number five out and re-grade your tests."

Grace sat back down, covering a little smile with a cough. Old Grace was getting her guts back. When Clay-

111

ton turned around to take papers from her, he whispered, "Thanks, Gracie."

She saw me watching and wrinkled her nose, but I know her and she likes Clayton. And besides, her cheeks were bright pink.

15

A Chip off the Old Block

Grace came and brought Matt. He seemed a little awkward in our house. "Sit down. Sit down," Mom said, and Matt sat on the edge of the couch, holding his can of Coke in one hand.

Grace sat on the floor with me, three feet from the TV. Willard had the VCR set for two minutes to six. It was four minutes to six. "I can't wait," Grace said. "I wonder what you'll look like."

"Like me," I said.

The last shot of Domino's Pizza left the screen. I sucked in my breath. There I was. Me and Nigel walking down the street. Nigel says, "Cancel all my Christmases. But just let me have that beauty for a week."

The camera moves to a close-up of my head as I turn to see what Nigel is talking about. The grin spreads over my face.

"Wow, you can even see your pumpkin teeth," Grace says.

I ram her in the side with my elbow to keep her quiet. I am saying on the screen, "Wow! That is one me-ean

113

machine." The camera pulls back to include the yellow convertible, which rolls by Nigel and me, and then the camera focuses on my face again to show my bug-eyed worship of the car.

The scene changes. A man in a business suit is standing in front of the yellow convertible saying, "You don't have to cancel all your Christmases to test-drive this beauty. In fact we'll give *you* a present if you visit Ted Dawson's Chrysler showroom for a . . ."

"Boy, that went fast," Grace said.

"But good." Matt tilted his Coke can to drink the last drops. "You ready to go, Gracie?"

"No, no. We can see it again on tape."

Willard rewound the cassette and switched the TV to the VCR.

Nigel and I are walking down the street. . . .

"I notice the camera stays on you more than on the other kid," Matt said to me.

I had noticed that too.

We watched Nigel and me two more times before Willard turned off the TV and shook my hand. "You came off like a pro, Jerry."

"Thanks," I said, and turned around to look at Mom.

Her eyes were swimming with tears. "Oh, you were just wonderful, honey."

Matt pulled Grace off the floor just as the phone rang. After Mom answered it, she held the receiver out to me. "It's your dad."

I said good-bye to Matt and Grace before I took the receiver and said hello to Dad.

"My boy, my boy, you knocked us dead."

"I tried," I said.

"Tried! You cleaned that other kid's clock."

"He gets hired for six or seven commercials a year."

"Not anymore," Dad said. "They've got a real actor now."

"I hope. How are things going with you?"

"Not bad. But I sure miss you. I wish I could have been along when you were shooting your commercial."

"I wish you could have too. It was fun."

"Maybe I'll be out in time for your second one. Unless they hire you again next week."

"I don't think I'll be that lucky."

"Oh, you can't tell. You're really good. You're the best I've ever seen."

"Thanks. And thanks for calling me, Dad."

After I hung up, I went into my bedroom thinking that I *was* a chip off the old block like he always said. He could make anybody believe anything. That is, anybody but the cops.

Grace and I had barely gotten on the morning bus when the guys in the back started yelling. "Hey, Johnson." "Hey, big shot, here's your seat." "Just 'cause you're on TV doesn't mean you're too good to sit with us."

Jenson and Taylor were back there with Clayton, hoping some of his cool would rub off on them, I guess. Jenson had crammed against Taylor to make room for me and was pounding on the empty space. Clayton just grinned.

All the guys slapped my hands when I went back to join them, and after I'd squeezed in, Taylor made a big show of rummaging around in his pockets with his one free arm. "I got a piece of paper here somewhere. I swear

115

I put it in my jacket this morning. Darn, it isn't here. Have to get your autograph later, Jackson. I mean Johnson."

"When's that commercial coming on again?" Clayton asked.

"I don't know. They only called to give me the time of the first one."

"Jeez, will all the babes be panting after you," Jenson said.

Pete was sitting on one of the side seats. I could tell he was listening even though he pretended to be looking out the window, and I wanted to mutter, just loud enough for him to hear, Eat your heart out, Pete.

When Jenson said that all the babes would be panting after me, I took it as some of his bull. It wasn't bull. I'd barely gotten to my locker when three girls crowded around me. "We heard you were on TV last night, Jerry."

"Um, ya, I was." What was there to say? I didn't even know the girls.

Grace walked up to them, holding her book bag to her chest. "Wasn't he great? I knew he would be. That's why I gave him the callboard for the commercial."

The blond girl wrinkled her forehead. "What's a callboard?"

Grace opened her mouth to explain, but Jenson came up behind her and gave her a shove. "Get lost, Holy Grace."

"Hey, wait a minute," I said. "Grace can—"

But before I could straighten Jenson out, a ninth-grade girl tugged on my arm. "You're Jerry Johnson, right?"

"Right," I agreed.

"I'm Jean Gomer. Ms. Castle suggested I interview

116

you for the school paper. Have you got a minute to answer a few questions?"

"I guess," I said.

She wanted to know how I spelled my name, what my address was, who I lived with, how long I'd been interested in acting, did I plan it for a career, and who had inspired me to act.

To answer the last question I said, "My dad, I guess. He was always a good actor and he used to a, um, put people on a lot and I went right along with him. I think I copied him without knowing and then when I started doing plays, it was easy."

The first bell rang, the kids scattered, Jean put her notebook in her purse and thanked me for the interview. While she'd been talking, I'd seen Summer start toward us, hesitate, and then walk down the hall. I nodded to Jean and sprinted after Summer. Too late. She'd disappeared into the home-ec room.

I stopped at her desk as soon as I got into history. "You passed right by my locker this morning."

Summer ducked her head. "I didn't want to bother you. You were busy."

"I'm not too busy for you."

Summer kept her head ducked and I noticed she also kept her hand over a spot on the cover of her notebook. Hmmm. I gave her hand a push. Two big initials, *J.J.* She must have drawn them over and over, because they looked like they were bleeding.

Her head was so far down now, I could only see her yellow hair. I pulled the pen out of her fingers and leaned over to print a *plus* and an *S.D.* under the *J.J.* Straightening up, I dropped my hand on the back of her neck. She lifted her head to look up at me. Out of the corner of my

117

eye I caught Grace coming into the room. I let go of Summer's neck and took my seat.

After Grace plunked her book bag on her desk, she sat down and huddled over it with that hangdog look. I should have pasted Jenson.

Beasley bustled in with our rescored tests. She had Kathy pass them out. "Heard you were on TV," Kathy whispered as she gave me my paper. She'd never bothered to whisper to me before.

The D-minus on my paper was crossed out and a big plain D was marked beside it. I looked across the aisle at Clayton's desk. He had his A.

Beasley started her lecture on the city of Everett, and I started wondering if the production company would give me another call. I did a little arithmetic on my desk. Five more jobs would buy me a decent car, even if I put twenty-five percent into Willard's fund. Ten more jobs would buy me a neat car. Twenty more jobs . . .

"What's this about TV?" Lonewolf asked me in PE.

"Oh, I just got a job in a commercial," I said.

"Let's have everybody sit down," Ms. Kraft yelled. "We're going to do a new dance."

Lonewolf and I sat on the floor together, legs crossed and chins on our hands.

"Now, watch me," Ms. Kraft said. She put a record on the turntable and glided out to the middle of the floor. "One, two, together, one, two, together, one, two, together. Who wants to be my partner?"

Lonewolf and I crouched lower.

"Come on, Angela. We'll show them how to waltz."

Angela heaved herself off the floor.

"One, two, together, one, two, together," Ms. Kraft sang out as she shoved and hauled Angela back and forth across the gym. "Come on, all of you. Stand up and try it by yourselves. One, two, together. Wait a minute. Wait a minute. Boys start with the left foot and girls start with the right foot. Okay, now! One, two, together, one, two, together, one, two . . ."

After Ms. Kraft figured we had the steps down, she announced a ladies' choice. Melissa and Kathy both made a beeline for me. Melissa won. Melissa's the most popular and prettiest and sappiest girl in the seventh grade. When Ms. Kraft called for a men's choice, I grabbed Clarice.

Nobody said anything to me about the commercial in shop. It was different in Ms. Castle's room, though. Right before the whole class she said, "You're lucky, J.J. The camera likes you."

What? The camera likes me?

She flipped her long hair back over her shoulder and laughed. "You have a 'wet face,' J.J. Everything shows on it."

Not everything. She didn't know all of me. "What's a 'wet face'?"

"A face that reflects emotions. An actor's face. And the camera loves it."

"Will it like mine?" Clarice asked.

Ms. Castle appraised Clarice carefully. "I think so. You have good eyes. Big. Expressive. And a wide smile." Ms. Castle nodded. "You should do fine."

"Johnson's got a hole between his two front teeth," Russell put in from the side of the room. You can talk out in Ms. Castle's class if a discussion is going on.

"Yes, he has a gap," Ms. Castle agreed. "But you don't want to be too perfect. An actor needs to look a little vulnerable so the audience can identify with him. Or

119

her." Ms. Castle smiled at Clarice. I was glad. I think Clarice can use a few smiles.

Grace could, too, but she wasn't taking any from me. I walked beside her on the trip home, jabbering away about the coming school dance, Clarice, and Ms. Castle. Grace interrupted, making it obvious that she was sick of hearing Ms. Castle's name. "What did that ninth-grade girl want?"

"She was asking me a bunch of questions for the school paper. She wanted to know my address and who I lived with and who had inspired me to act. That kind of junk."

"Who did you say inspired you?"

"I told her my dad had, that he was a good actor, and I took after him."

"You could have left him out of it. Lots of kids know he's in prison."

"No way," I said. "I'm not hiding stuff about my dad anymore."

Grace glanced at me. Her face was pale and sad. "I guess you can get away with anything now."

"Maybe. But if I'd faced it before, it would have saved me a lot of sweating."

She just shrugged.

When we came to her walkway, I suggested, "I might come over later."

She shrugged again.

You blew it, Johnson, I told myself as I went on to my house. You should have stuck up for her when you had the chance.

I wolfed down a sandwich, turned on the TV in case my commercial came on, and walked into my bedroom to dump my books. I was thinking I'd go over to Grace's anyway and try to make her feel better. But when I got to her driveway, I heard crying. Instead of going to the front door, I eased around toward the back.

As I rounded the bushes by the porch, I saw her crouched on the steps crying in a way I'd never seen before. Her head and shoulders heaved with long, gasping, heartbroken sobs. Before I could get to her, Matt came out the back door. He sat on the step beside her.

"Don't cry, Gracie," he said. "Dad'll make Mom change her mind. He spends so much time counseling, she hardly sees him, and she takes her frustration out on you."

"It . . . it doesn't matter."

"Sure it matters. You won't have to go in one of those granny dresses. It's just that girls didn't wear jeans to dances when Mom was young."

"It . . . it won't make any difference even if I am in jeans. No one will dance with me."

"Sure they will. Come on, Gracie, don't cry anymore." Matt fished around in his pockets.

"You don't understand. Some of the kids hate me now. They say, 'Get out of here, Holy Grace.' Like I'm a dog or something. It . . . it hurts."

Matt drew back a little as if he'd been hurt too. Then he seemed to pull himself together and got the handkerchief out of his pocket. While he dabbed at her tears, I silently faded away from their driveway, across my lawn, and into my back door.

If it hadn't been for Grace, I'd never have been on TV. I'll make it up to her, I promised myself. I'll get us a ride to the dance and dance with her, and if Jenson and Taylor make any cracks, this time I'll deck them.

121

16

The End of Holy Grace

Grace didn't go to school the rest of the week. When her mother answered my knocks on their door, she looked a bit green. She told me the family had come down with the flu.

I didn't worry about Grace much during the week because I figured she'd be well for the dance on Saturday. I kept my TV on from the time I got home after school until I went to bed. It wasn't until Thursday night, though, that I saw my commercial again. I was in the kitchen eating when I heard, "Me-ean machine."

It sounded like me. It was me! I jumped out of my chair so fast I spilled milk all over the tablecloth. I made it to the living room in time to see the close-up of the car.

In the halls at school I heard the words *mean machine* over and over again, but I kept walking as if I didn't notice. The school newspaper got delivered to Beasley's class on Friday. Some kid came in and dumped a stack of them on her desk. Beasley said we could read them at the end of the hour if we paid attention until then. I paid attention.

123

My interview was across the bottom of the first page, just below Ratch's article on how to behave at a school dance. Quotation marks were around the part where I'd said my dad was a good actor and I'd copied him. Summer whispered, "I bet your dad will be proud."

Summer's always been nice about my dad, but I was still a little worried about the other kids. I guess I didn't have to be. When I stood in the hot-lunch line that day, Kathy and Melissa were giggling behind me. I turned around and saw that they each had a school paper.

"Hi, Mean Machine." Kathy gave me a grin full of wires.

"New braces, huh?" I said.

She slapped her hand over her lips and nodded, red with embarrassment.

"Are you going to the school dance?" Melissa asked.

"Maybe," I said.

Saturday morning I asked Mom if she'd give me and Grace a ride to the dance.

"Sure," she said.

Willard was heading for the bedroom to get dressed for work. He stopped dead at the kitchen door. "You aren't going to be at the restaurant tonight?"

"Yes, but I can take a half hour off to drive Jerry to the junior high."

Willard frowned. "It'll take more than a half hour."

Mom didn't answer him. She was busy reading my interview in the school paper. Willard heaved a sigh, but it didn't get him any attention, so he went on through the door.

Mom put the paper down and took a sip of her coffee.

Her eyes were all misty. "What a sweet thing to say about your dad, honey." She took another sip. "You know, he was the most fun and the most loving man I ever knew."

She was right and after she went to work, I walked over to Grace's house thinking about Mom and Dad and Willard. If Mom took the neat parts of Dad and the super-straight, hardworking parts of Willard, she'd have a whole man. Grace answered my knock on her door.

"Hi," I said cheerfully. "You're over the flu."

She managed to say hi back, but she didn't look too happy.

"What're you doing?"

"Helping my mom."

"You going to the dance tonight?"

"I don't know."

"My mom's driving. Why don't you ride with us?"

"No, Matt'll take me."

I leaned against the doorjamb and gave her another smile. "There's no point in two cars driving to school. You might as well go with us. I might even dance with you."

"No, if I go, Matt promised Mom he'd take me and pick me up. Thanks for asking me anyway." She closed the door.

Shaking my head, I walked slowly down her porch steps, across her yard, and over to my mailbox. I should have stood up for her.

Mixed in with the mess of bills was a letter from Dad. I ripped open the envelope as I went up my front steps and into my house. His letter was mostly about how he felt when he and the other prisoners watched my commercial. "When your commercial came on, I said to all

125

the guys, 'That's my boy! That's my boy!' Jerry, I can't ever remember being so proud."

I stood in the middle of our living room imagining him alone in his cell. Maybe he never would make it on the outside, but, as Mom said, he was a loving man. Sometimes having him for a dad had seemed like the worst thing that ever happened to me. And sometimes the best.

I tossed his letter and the bills on the coffee table. From the drawer in the kitchen I got scissors. And from Mom's room I got a stamp and envelope. I cut the interview out of my newspaper, circled the part about who inspired me, and wrote in the margin, "Dear Dad, I mean this. Love, Jerry." If he was proud before, he was really going to burst when he opened this letter.

There was pink crepe paper looped across the ceiling of the gym, pink balloons hanging from the basketball nets, and pink paper flowers tied with pink bows to the walls. Three girls in pink blouses stood in back of the punch bowl. One of them was a seventh-grader. "You seen Grace Elliott around?" I asked her.

"Nope," she said.

The girl stirring the pink punch asked me if I wanted some.

"I don't know." I took a couple sniffs over the bowl. "What does it taste like?"

"It's good. Strawberry." She ladled some into a paper cup and handed it to me.

I took a taste. "It is good," I agreed. All three girls looked pleased with themselves.

I eased myself around clumps of kids and over to the

side wall, where I saw Ms. Castle standing with Ms. Kraft. "You're the chaperons," I said.

"*She* is," Ms. Kraft said. "I'm the DJ and I'd better get the music started." She went over to the long table under the basketball hoop and started sorting through a stack of cassettes.

"The school poor or something?" I asked Ms. Castle.

Ms. Castle laughed. "No, she just likes doing things with you kids."

"Couldn't she stick to coaching baseball?"

"Don't worry. I gave her some of my tapes to mix in with hers."

"Choose your partners!" Ms. Kraft called out. "The first dance is coming up." She snapped a cassette into the recorder, and the Beach Boys blared from the speakers behind her.

"Yuck," a girl standing by me said.

I was careful not to say anything, because it could be Ms. Castle's tape. I watched the kids waving their arms to the music for a couple of seconds while I tried to get up the courage to ask Ms. Castle for a dance. She was wearing a slinky green dress with a slit in the skirt, and my hands were sweating.

I'd just wiped them down the legs of my jeans and had taken in a breath to ask her to dance, when I realized her face had lit up for a guy coming through the gym doors. The guy was about five feet six and wore black-rimmed glasses.

"Teddy, you made it after all," she said to him when he'd reached her.

Teddy?

"We finished early." He took a strand of her auburn

127

hair and tucked it behind her ear. He had little hands. Little white hands.

"I'll see ya," I mumbled, and made for the hall, where I dumped my cup in the trash can and took a drink of water out of the fountain. I'd expected her to pick someone better than *Teddy*.

Two eighth-grade girls walked past me. "Me-ean machine," one said to the other. I ignored them.

By the time I got back in the gym, Ms. Kraft had managed some rock. I looked carefully around the dancers. Summer should be in there somewhere.

I didn't see Summer, but I did see Grace. She was standing against the wall all by herself in her jeans and black vest. Her chin was tilted up and her eyes were glazed. A red spot of embarrassment flamed on each cheek.

I sidled up beside her. "Guess what? I just beat the crap out of Jenson."

She jerked around to face me. "You didn't!"

"No, but I will if you want me to."

She couldn't help herself. She had to laugh.

Kathy and Melissa danced up close to us. "Hi, Jerry," Kathy said.

"Your braces hurt?" I asked her.

"No." She snapped her mouth closed and moved away.

"That wasn't nice," Grace said.

"So? She didn't remember my name until I was on TV."

"Well." Grace shrugged. "She's like that."

"Come on. Let's finish this dance." I put my hand on her back and pushed her away from the wall. By the time the music stopped, she was pretty loose.

We watched Ms. Kraft rummage through her tapes. "Ah," she said into the microphone. "Here's an oldie but goodie. You can dance the Charleston to this. Anybody know the Charleston?"

"Oh, I do," Grace said to me.

"You do?"

"My uncle who had the *Seattle Weekly* taught me how."

"Show me," I said.

"No, not here."

"Come on. I've never seen it."

"Well." She ripped at her fingernail and scrinched up her face, the old Grace fighting with the sad Grace.

I gave her a shove. "Do it!"

She did. She bent down, crossed her hands over her knees, and twirled her feet. As the music speeded up, so did Grace. One foot after the other screwed into the floor while one leg after the other flew out to the side.

Whoa, I couldn't follow that. I just shuffled around, watching Grace go for it. Clayton and Summer danced near us. "Aw right, Gracie!" Clayton yelled above the music.

Grace heard. I could tell because she missed a beat. But she kept on going until the music stopped.

"I'm hot. Let's get some punch." The two red spots had turned to a rosy flush, and her black curls were sticking to her face.

The girls in charge of refreshments had left filled cups around the bowl. Grace emptied one in two gulps.

Jenson and Taylor moved up to the table. "Jeez, it's hot in this place," Jenson said.

Grace picked up another cup. "Here, I'll cool you off." And she poured the punch right over his head.

He backed up, gasping. "You little witch!"

There were two kids at the end of the table and they cracked up, which made Jenson even madder. I thought I was going to be in a fight for sure, but Clayton and Summer came across the floor just as the music started. Clayton clapped a hand on Jenson's shoulder. "What's going on? You're all wet."

Jenson wiped his forehead with his sleeve and jabbed a finger toward Grace. "This—"

"Gracie! Dance with me!" Clayton took one of her hands to bring her to him and then circled his arms around her waist. She shot me a wide-eyed glance before she glided out onto the floor.

Jenson's mouth hung open as he watched her go. Taylor kept shaking his head as if he couldn't believe what was happening.

I turned to Summer. "Dance with me?"

After we'd taken a few steps, she looked up into my face. "What's funny?"

"Jenson and Taylor just found out they've been putting down the wrong girl."

It was a slow tune, and at first I held Summer loosely in my arms. But gradually our swaying to the music together made me braver and I drew her closer. She felt as soft as I'd imagined. I brought her closer still until my hand was on the back of her neck and her downy yellow hair brushed my chin.

I caught a glimpse of Grace through the crowd. She didn't looked wide-eyed anymore. Her arms were around Clayton, her head was tilted back, and she was smiling at him as they circled around the room. Holy Grace, I guessed, was dead.

Barthe DeClements is the author of several award-winning novels for children and young adults, including the best-selling *Nothing's Fair in Fifth Grade* and *Sixth Grade Can Really Kill You.* In addition to writing, she has also worked as a psychologist, a teacher, and a school counselor. Her most recent novel for Delacorte Press was *Monkey See. Monkey Do.*, the sequel to *Five-Finger Discount. Breaking Out* completes the trilogy.

Barthe DeClements has four grown children and two pet wolf hybrids. She lives in a log house on the Pilchuck River near Snohomish, Washington.